Starting Over

By

Charmaine Gordon

Vanilla Heart Publishing

Starting Over

by Charmaine Gordon

Copyright 2011 Charmaine Gordon

Published by: Vanilla Heart Publishing
www.VanillaHeartBookAndAuthors.com
10121 Evergreen Way, 25-156
Everett, WA 98204 USA

ISBN-13: 978-0615909165 ISBN-10: 0615909167

10 9 8 7 6 5 4 3 2 Second Edition

First Printing, October 2013
Printed in the United States of America

Starting Over

By

Charmaine Gordon

Dedication

Once upon a time, someone said, (maybe it was me) "when you learn the dance of life, learn it well. When things go south, take one step forward, slide two steps back; two steps forward, one step back.

Here comes the biggie. It's called the hesitation step. Little step forward, longer step

forward, giant steps ahead."

This story is dedicated to everyone with the courage to learn the dance of life.

Acknowledgements

When "Read a story, Mommy," became "Make up a story, Mom," writing seeds were planted and didn't blossom until years later. I thank my family for the early years when

life was less complex and sometimes, children paid attention.

In this far different time, a new friend, Kimberlee Williams, called and said, "Tell me a story." And I did. An idea buried deep poured out with her encouragement and I wrote and wrote.

Enjoy the journey of Starting Over, dear Reader.

Chapter 1

She ran as fast as she could on the hard packed sand this early morning in February, still cold in St. Augustine, Florida. Cold and beautiful with the tide out and no one around. Almost always surefooted, not as steady since Larry died eight months before, Emily Kendrick stumbled and caught her balance. There was a sense of someone watching her, close to her, yet she ran into no one on the deserted beach. It was almost an everyday occurrence. Tears spilled down her face just as the hurdles set for the track team came up. Easy leap over the first one, the second knocked over by a careless foot. Emily fell and didn't get up.

A lone runner sprinted through the waves and hurried to aid the fallen woman.

Binoculars slammed against the railing of the widow's walk where two eyes had been watching the long-legged runner for months. From his well hidden perch high up on the mansion overlooking the Atlantic Ocean, under investigation the infamous Clifford Lansdale said, "She's mine." Fragments of the expensive binoculars lay at his feet.

"Are you all right?" the runner said.

Emily laughed and cried. "Oh sure. I never stumble like this and the kids will be coming down for practice soon. I've got to be on top of my game to train them." She stood up, checked all her parts to make sure nothing was damaged and brushed off sand. "Thanks for stopping by. I'm Emily Kendrick." She noticed the runner checking out all her parts too and shook her head. Guys. They just can't help it.

"Patrick Corwin. What kids?"

"I coach the women's track team at the college. We're at the beach most days before the crowd." She opened a thermos and offered tea. Patrick begged off.

"I run early before office hours. Have to get up to Jacksonville before morning rush." He fished a business card from his running shorts. "Call me. I'd enjoy getting to know you better, Emily."

Patrick left before she had a chance to say no. How could she ever go out with another man? Larry was the best husband in the world, her high school sweetie. Emily didn't know how she was going to spend the rest of her life without him. Their children were grown up and married. They loved her but had their own lives to lead. "Go out, Mom," Tommy said. "Have some fun. Dad wouldn't want you to be alone." Her daughter wasn't eager for her to date. "Play Bridge, learn how to use the computer we bought you. I'll have a baby for you to play with." Emily hated card games, computers were scary, babies sounded wonderful but is that how life would be?

From sounds of a bus coming over the nearby dune, Emily knew the team had arrived. Time to work and work was the answer for now. After a grueling two hour work-out, the sweating pony-tail crowd waved goodbye to the coach and headed back to school. Emily pedaled her way up the beach to the lovely old house with the wrap-around porch purchased thirty years before when beach front property was affordable.

The mail and paper were dumped on a table purchased years before to accommodate a family of four, now too big for one person. She poured hot decaf coffee over one packet of sweetener and sighed as she sat down on the old captain's chair. The rubber band slipped down easily and Emily sorted the mail, bills in one stack, discount coupons for cleaning, movies, and food in another. Ready to fling the pizza delivery flyer in the garbage, she reconsidered with a shrug of her shoulders and placed it in the second pile. A catalog for men's clothes went flying, followed by one with seductive lingerie for sale. Emily retrieved it just in case she lived long enough to change her mind about dating.

She slowly made her way to the big mirror in the hall and looked at the gray roots, the few wrinkles, and shook her head. Emily Kendrick, femme fatale. A woman with grown children and no husband. At her age. Fifty something. Too scary.

The glass is half full. Got it? Stop feeling sorry for yourself. Time to take charge of your life. Yes, you're a coach and phys ed teacher but it's time to buckle down and learn a new skill like the dreaded computer. Everyone uses one. Why not me? Take a course and learn.

A quick call to the college and she learned that a beginner course in computers was starting in a few weeks. Before she could change her mind, Emily signed up, credit card information over the phone. Sashaying over to the dusty laptop computer box, she cleaned it off and said,"Hey pal, you and I are going to get acquainted."

Unaware that the stalker had taken up his position in his hiding place, Emily made plans for the afternoon. Clifford Lansdale knew Emily Kendrick's schedule.

After a quick lunch and shower, Emily biked over to the swim and tennis club where water aerobics classes were held. Her closest friends hung out there most afternoons.

Margaret treaded water and waved hello. Shelly was in the deep end beginning laps and Jesse sat in a lounge chair, clip board in hand, pen poised as she planned something wonderful from the look on her face. Emily plopped down next to Jesse. "What are you up to? You look like the cat that swallowed the proverbial canary."

With a haughty expression, Jesse said, "I am planning a get-together right here at the swim club. It's a membership drive so we're going to have a luau theme, music, dancing, great food and people will stand in line to join. What do you think, Emily?"

"Terrific." Emily dived in and swam laps with Shelly.

"Jesse told you about the membership drive party?"

"Uh huh."

"Discount next year's dues if you bring in new meat."

"Nicely put."

"What about that widower friend. Maybe he'd like to join."

Emily thought about her old friend, Mark Wagner. She and Larry were best friends with Mark and Sally. When both Sally and Larry had died within a year of each other, Emily thought maybe she and Mark would get together. But no. They had one dinner and he never called. She hadn't heard from him in months. She hoped he wouldn't join the club. On the other hand, it might be an opportunity to get together.

She dried off and called his office.

"Lenore, this is Emily Kendrick. May I speak with Himself for a sec?" She envisioned Lenore frowning, then giving in.

"Hold please."

Emily picked at her nail polish as she waited. Taking too long for Mark to respond was not a good sign.

A click and Lenore said, "Emily, I'm sorry but—"

"He said too busy. He said later. Right?"

"Right."

"Thanks anyway." Emily hung up.

She wallowed in self-pity for a while and returned to the pool.

Early the next morning, Emily was back on the beach. Running, running, running. Years of running. Waves lapped greedily at the shore as if they knew the time for tide in would come soon and they could pounce, white caps slap–slap as they rose higher and higher. Patrick Corwin raised a hand in greeting from a distance. Nice looking man, runner's shape, lean and mean. And he was fast. Suddenly he was next to Emily, slowing down a bit to keep pace. How kind.

"You don't have to slow down for me."

"Want to."

They ran in companionable silence. Out of the blue, Emily said, "If you're free next Saturday night, would you like to go to a terrific party? It's a membership drive for the swim and tennis club on the beach." She babbled on. "It's a friendly club. My family's belonged there for a long time. There'll be good food, good people, and I think, good conversation. I'll meet you there. All you have to do is show up. It starts at seven Saturday night."

She gave him the full batting-eyelash treatment. He agreed to go and ran off, a big smile on his face.

At home, she thought about what she'd accomplished on her own. She actually invited a guy to a party. Wow! She may not be one who balances a checkbook or calls the plumber or mechanic because there was more authority when a male voice called. Isn't that what she was brought up to believe? All her friends believed that too. Well, there wasn't a male voice in her household anymore so she better learn to make her own calls. But the headline today was Emily Kendrick had the guts to invite a man to a club to invite a man to a club party—no strings attached. Or were there

Chapter 2

Saturday, after two hours in and out of her closet trying on different outfits, she settled on a flowered long sleeved shirt tied at the waist, white silk pants, and sandals. Her sun streaked light brown hair was blown straight. Not easy being single. The mirror reflected an attractive, slim, energetic woman. The grieving widow was in disguise.

Emily drove to the club in her Jeep. Margaret hurried to greet Emily.

"The guy, the handsome lawyer, Patrick Corwin's been asking for you. Yum. Where'd you meet him?"

"Running on the beach. Where is he?"

She pointed him out.

Taking a deep breath, Emily walked over, dressed in what she called civilian clothes, to say hello. Patrick looked mighty nice, all cleaned up. The phrase, clean him up and send him to my tent came to mind. A deep flush stained her tan cheeks.

"Hi, Patrick." Smooth, Emily.

He held a paper plate topped with fresh shrimp on skewers.

"I love shrimp."

"I love to share."

So far, so good. The shrimp was tasty, Emily's friends thought her new friend was also tasty and he not only was a runner but a good dancer. They danced. She hadn't been in anyone's arms but Larry's in many years. New adventures. Patrick even joined the club. Discount membership for Emily. What an evening.

They sat outside for a while, Tiki torches fired up, the band let loose with Calypso music, waves pounded the shore, and stars were close enough to touch. A night meant for romance. Not for Emily without Larry or maybe there was a future on a night like this. She wondered as Patrick held her hand.

His blue eyes were sad. He pulled her close, not too close He smelled good. Seemed sincere. Tricky business, this man-woman thing at her age. Whom can you trust, she wondered. Trust me, his eyes pleaded.

"You are newly single"? She nodded. "Will it upset you if I explain some basic safety rules about being single?"

"No, go ahead," she said and wondered why she felt like a dumb, helpless female.

And she didn't mind his take-charge attitude. In fact, she kind of liked it. After Patrick's safety lecture, they spent the rest of the evening playing what Emily called getting-to-know-you. She hadn't done that since she was a teenager, but it all came back as if it were yesterday. Too soon it was time to say goodnight. Patrick said, "Do you have a cell phone?"

"Why do you ask?" A funny question from this intense man she'd been with for several hours.

He persisted. "Do you?"

"I forgot to charge the battery. It's at home on the charger." Emily found her wrap, slipped it on, and turned to him. "If this is a test, did I fail?" She grinned.

He removed the tinniest cell phone she had ever seen from an inside pocket of his jacket, flipped it open, keyed in 911, and placed it in her hand. The musk scent of his after shave lotion distracted her.

"Emily, pay attention." Startled, she did. "Hold this in your left hand as you drive. Be aware at all times of where you are, what street, what town."

"Seems overly cautious to me. I'm driving straight home just a few blocks away." Emily felt uneasy. Why was Patrick so protective of her? Already he was territorial about her. "I appreciate your advice, but I can't —"

His finger touched her mouth. She tried to give the phone back but he shook his head.

"I'll get it next time we meet." His eyes never left hers. She broke eye contact first.

"I'll call you soon." She fumbled for her wrap and bag. "We'll make a plan."

Something about those blue eyes intrigued her.

He smiled and said, "Yes."

"Yes what?"

"Yes, you'll call me. Soon."

Patrick escorted her outside. He kissed her cheek and whispered in her ear. "Goodnight, my little sweetheart. See you on the beach"

When he breathed in her ear, she felt a tingle she'd missed since her husband died. A glow from the pleasant evening warmed her until she turned into her street and the good mood changed. Grief dragged at her spirit. It was always like that, coming home to an empty dark house. She must remember to leave some lights on. She wondered when the grief would stop haunting her, the way it showed up unexpected like an uninvited guest.

Chapter 3

Visions of lost power invaded his dreams. He thrashed and moaned, waking, skin damp with sweat, sheets in a tangle.

For years his wife had nagged him. "Did you take your pills? You know how you are when you don't take your pills." He was the boss around here. How dare anyone tell him what to do.

"Delusions of grandeur, my ass." he said. "What's this Bipolar shit they keep talking about?"

He listened to his zillion dollar house. Just the ocean to talk to. Good. And his lawyer. Soon. And the Judge. They said he was going down. Not if he could help it.

He jumped out of bed and swept everything off the dresser. Bottles went flying, pills tumbled through the air, framed pictures crashed, glass shattering everywhere. And he stood there not moving, amidst the chaos he created. A man of sixty years, hair askew. Still not bad. He sucked in his gut. "Got to meet that beauty before it's too late. The runner on the beach, the man, looks familiar. Zoom in on him," he said to himself.

Chapter 4

Emily undressed, careful to hang the party clothes in her walk-in closet. There was a dumb game she played, alone in her bedroom. How long could the widow avert her eyes from the empty closet next to hers. If she opened the door one more time and saw hangers without clothes, shoe racks without shoes, would she cry? She spent three hours in close conversation with a man tonight. Maybe it was time to move some of her belongings to the second closet. Claim it for her own.

Reaching into the shower, she turned on the faucet and waited for the water to run hot. Adjustments made, she stepped under the spray and poured shampoo on already clean hair.

"Idiot. What the hell are you doing?" she yelled out loud.

A rich lather formed from the excess shampoo. No need for soap tonight. As she washed body and hair, she thought about Patrick. Rewound their conversation and played it back in her head. As water rinsed off the foamy suds, she thought about Patrick again. Was he a man to be trusted? He was guarded about his background, revealing just enough for her to peek. His marriage wasn't a happy one. He didn't admit it to his credit but she added up the few comments and came to that conclusion. He was crazy about his newly married daughter. He was a lawyer involved in a big case right now. No reason to lie about any of those facts.

Her body felt different somehow. For months she'd felt dried up, afraid of crumbling to dust. The joyful moist feeling that was a big part of her marriage was gone. Meeting Patrick tonight offered some hope for a return to that happy state. His kiss, the breath in her ear warmed places she had almost forgotten about. Could there be orgasms in her future? She hoped so. She wasn't naïve. She'd read about pleasuring herself in self-help books, but hey guys, it wasn't the same. Nothing like the warmth of clean skin next to you. Turned her right on. Larry used to come to bed without taking a shower and she'd point to the bathroom. He'd hurry back still damp and—ooh baby. Reaching up to switch the showerhead to massage, she remembered that Larry's hand was the last to use that adjustment. She stroked and patted the nozzle. How he loved the pounding needles of water. She whispered, "Larry, I miss you so much. We had good times in this shower." Slowly Emily turned under the cascade, tears falling, hands soothing her skin, and felt alive with the possibility of a future.

Her stream of consciousness and the hot water gave out at the same time. Wrapped in a fluffy towel, she rubbed steam off the bathroom clock. Oh God. One in the morning already. Dry your hair and go to bed.

As Emily fell asleep, her last thought was, I'll call him. Yes, I will.

Chapter 5

Patrick Corwin drove fast. He covered the ten miles to his condominium in five minutes. Brakes squealed, car door slammed, long strides and he was in his home, in the bedroom, jacket still on. Light snapped on in the closet, he got down on all fours, crawled to the back, and groped for a metal box. Heart hammering, he found the elusive key on his key chain and unlocked the box. Removing a journal, he unlocked it with another key, and lifted the pen inside the book. He sat on the floor of the organized closet filled with suits, shirts, shoes for every occasion, and clothes from school days he refused to part with, and wrote in his journal.

March 1st

Met THE woman tonight after a ten year search. I'm not good enough for her. Will try to protect her from harm for the rest of my life.

He reread the terse entry. Pen replaced, journal locked and set in the box, box locked and shoved into the depth of the closet. Can't be too cautious. He crawled out, removed and hung up his clothes. Everything in place. Bed embraced his exhausted body in the indentation made by too many restless nights and too many secrets. Why did he ever take this case? He clutched a worn brown plaid quilt in his fist, burrowed in, and slept a dreamless sleep.

Chapter 6

"Emily, this better be important or you owe me big time," Jesse said, with an early morning unused-as-yet voice.

Emily fidgeted on the bed. "Sorry. Were you guys sleeping or—oh shit. I interrupted something, didn't I? What a jerk. Sorry. Please forgive me. I'll give you my firstborn and—"

Muffling a laugh, Jesse whispered, "No, we just finished, he rolled off and is on his way downstairs to make coffee for the little woman. I was a good girl." They giggled. "Why the hell are you calling so early and on a Sunday yet. You know we always do it on Sunday mornings even when Ken has golf or whatever."

"Sorry, sorry, sorry. Listen to this. I met a man last night and I'm wearing a path through my carpet with the pacing back and forth. I can't decide whether or not to call him today and I need advice from my best pal and—her line was busy so I called you." Emily waited while Jesse laughed her head off. "What do you think?"

"I think you're out of your mind. That's for starters."

"A simple yes or no will do. I don't want a lecture." Impatient, Emily jumped up and paced. "Come on."

"Call him. Whatever I say, you're going to call him anyway." Kat hung up.

She said yes, she did. Great. Emily speed dialed back. "Once a week you do it?" and hung up, leaving an echo of laughter in Kat's ear.

Time crept by as Emily stretched, went for the Sunday run, ate breakfast, watched the clock-still too early to call, tidied the kitchen and it was 10 a.m. The time was right. Apprehensive about being pushy, clammy with anticipation or maybe she just needed a shower, she dialed his number and hung up. Still uncertain, she pictured her single friend Lola in the same situation. Lola, every hair in place even when she painted, dressed to perfection. When they first became friends, she clued Emily in on certain rules. There were none. "See what you like and go after it," she said. "If you don't, someone else will. We're talking women, honey, competition. More of us out there than men, so don't waste time. Not like when you grew up".

Inhaling a deep breath, Emily exhaled and dialed again. His business card looked worn from sweaty palms and too much handling in less than a day.

"Hi." She cleared her throat. "It's Emily. Remember me?"

"Remember you? I can't get you out of my head. I want to see you. Now," Patrick said.

Nice. Cheeks flushed at his words. "How about dinner tonight or should that be your line?" she said. Her body felt warm from head to toe. Beads of sweat formed across her forehead.

"How about dinner now?"

A sharp intake of breath, take it slow. Emily shook her head. "It's morning, too early for dinner, isn't it?" You're giving him an opening that can't be closed.

"Not for me. Directions to your home, please."

She threw all caution away and told him. No turning back, Ms. Emily.

In a frenzy, amazed at her audacity, she changed the sheets, and paid attention to herself. What to wear? Dress like a slut? That's how you feel. No. Be yourself. What am I? I don't know. Her body aglow with anticipation, she was out of control.

A quick shower, perfume applied in all the right places, makeup on. She moved close to the mirror. No blush needed today, cheeks rosy. Finger-combed ash brown hair, sun streaks blended with gray. She slipped into a lacy black pushup bra and panty set–oh Emily it's eleven in the morning– skinny jeans and a silk burgundy sweater. No. She changed into comfortable undies, shorts and a pullover sweater. Take it slow, you fool. No matter what he wants, you're the boss.

The door bell rang. A final glance in the mirror and ready or not, she flew down the stairs. Ms. Hard-to-get. She paused to catch her breath and with an attempt at poise, she opened the door.

Patrick, even better looking by day–more rugged, was dressed much like her. He kissed her cheek and asked her to show him around her to old beach house. Calming down, Emily gave him a royal tour of the charming home with a great ocean view.

"Nice," he said. "I've never owned a home. I, uh, grew up in the Midwest and we moved around a lot. When I was married, well—it was only a short time."

She took his hand and led him upstairs.

"Beautiful," he said, looking at her. He gestured to the empty closet. "This was your husband's closet."

"Yes."

"Looks comfortable," he said, sitting on the chaise lounge she used for reading in comfort, his dark masculinity a sharp contrast to the feminine pastel fabric. "This is a wonderful home. Excuse me for saying this but I feel your husband wants you to be fulfilled, to have pleasure."

"How do you know?" Emily said, surprised at the turn of conversation.

"If I were him, that's what I'd want." Patrick rose and took her hand. "Let's go to the Conch House for lunch."

At some point during lunch, Patrick leaned forward and said, "Trust me. I promise I will never hurt you."

Chapter 7

The Conch House, overlooking the waterway, was a well known restaurant. As natives of the area, Emily and her family had dined there many times over the years. Greeted warmly by Susan, the hostess of the afternoon, they were seated outside under a canopy.

"How long have you been here?" said Patrick.

"I grew up close by. And how long have you been here? I never saw you before the day you came to my rescue."

He smiled. "Not too long. I live in a condo about twenty miles north of town. I'm a lawyer working on one case right now. Complicated. What's good?" he said, referring to the menu.

He'd changed the subject. Emily guessed it was too confidential. "I told you I love shrimp so anything with shrimp."

They ordered shrimp salad and iced tea, a typical light lunch for Emily.

The sea breeze caressed her cheeks; the sun peeked in and out of billowing white clouds enough not to burn. Something about sunshine on her body stirred sleeping pheromones. She felt Patrick's eyes on her.

"What?" she said.

"I'd love to kiss you right now."

The waiter brought lunch just as Emily was about to respond and the moment passed.

"Tell me about yourself." Emily said, after the waiter left.

He tasted the shrimp, murmured that it was fine, and thought. "Okay. Born and raised in the mid west, speak a bunch of languages, married a young woman who died in Israel when I worked there. One daughter married. I raised her with help from close —friends. Case closed." He flashed a grin. "Your turn."

"Oh. My life has been more mundane. Married forever to my high school sweetie who died not long ago, raised two children both married. I coach track and work as phys ed teacher at the college and am about to learn computer skills just because it's a challenge."

As they left the restaurant, Emily realized her first date was more than pleasant. She'd like to see Patrick again and from the glances he gave her throughout lunch, he'd like to see more of her. Her cheeks flushed red. How much more of her would be revealed before too soon. She had no idea how romances proceeded in this time so different from the 'olden days' when most girls were virgins before marriage. One step at a time and always remember, you're the boss when it comes to matters of the heart—and body.

Patrick was way ahead of her.

"What are you blushing about, Emily? Are you wondering what comes next?"

They both laughed and it was fun to bring the big question out in the open.

"Caught in the act. I'm new at this dating thing, as you know, so?"

"We'll go slow and see how we fit together."

That brought another burst of laughter and the afternoon came to a close.

Chapter 8

Eyes burned through the zoom on the binoculars."Son of a bitch. It's him, Patrick Corwin. Traitor. My own lawyer hired to serve and protect me. Kissing my Goddess. What else is he doing to her? Son of a bitch." Binoculars smashed again and again chipping the railing of the widow's walk. He wanted to crush the traitor's throat with his bare hands, feel him gasp for breath, watch life fade from his clever lawyer's eyes."Not yet. I need his expertise to clear my good name." Clifford Lansdale laughed and drank another cup of black coffee.

Chapter 9

Tide came in earlier these mornings but the couple on the beach stopped running and stood entwined in the swirling water as romance grew. Soon passion could not be denied. Patrick pressed his tightening groin to Emily's heat.

"I can't run another step," he said."How about you?"

Eyes closed, she caught her breath."I have to teach soon. Later? Come over for, uh, dinner?"

"Okay. One more kiss?"

Emily shook her head no."I hear the bus. See you later."

An attempt at dinner failed. They couldn't keep their hands off each other. The gentlemanly Patrick almost tore off her shirt and when he saw her bra, he said,"I love lace," and traced her nipples through the delicate fabric until she unhooked and let him taste the tender tips. Then the white shorts were peeled down and Emily stepped out revealing matching lace panties. Patrick slowly dropped down to his knees and whispered,"Ah, the main course." The lovers giggled and soon Emily gasped as he dipped his tongue in the sweetest spot of all."Hold onto my shoulders, Sweetheart."

Pat was naked next to her, inside her too soon because they couldn't wait a moment longer and so it went. Crying out her name, Patrick shuddered and Emily joined him in a crescendo of sexual love. The joyful tingle and release over and over again like honeymooners at last lulled them to sleep.

Hours later, Emily cried out.

"It's me, Emily. Don't be afraid. I have to leave and couldn't resist one last hug."

The room was dark. The last thing she remembered was having the best orgasms ever followed by kisses and loves and now he was dressed and ready to go and she'd be alone again. Somehow she never thought about the end of the evening. She wondered if he left money on the dresser. Like, thanks for a swell time, lady. Maybe he'd call some other time at his convenience. She felt cheap, a tramp, an easy woman. Naked under the blanket and he's dressed in leathers. God.

Soft kisses on her cheek. "Be gone all week on business but I'll try to call every day, if that's okay with you." Caresses under the blanket."You'll be in my thoughts, little sweetheart."

She felt his weight on the bed, the warmth of him nearby. The scent of her shampoo rose from his hair, vanilla body wash lingered on his skin, evidence he'd showered while she slept. How did he know she loved clean skin? In response, she arched her back to get closer, to press against him. She couldn't help it. Hormones long asleep were awake wanting more, like a teenager.

"Give me your face, your mouth," she said and thrust her tongue deep, round and round, in and out the way he did when he was on top in her center.

His breathing grew rapid, matching hers. She heard zippers unzip, boots kicked off, and they were joined a moment later. So good. Oh yes. So randy, it didn't take long to finish. Now he had to leave. She knew he'd come back.

As he dressed again, he said,"You need more secure locks on the doors, front and back, until an alarm system is installed."

Was this his concept of post-coital conversation? Emily sat up and knocked on his back."Hello. What are you talking about?"

A tug on each boot, he stood ready to leave."I want to protect you, dearest Emily," and headed for the door.

"From what? I've been here thirty years, same house, same locks, and always felt safe."

Patrick covered the distance to the bed in a few long strides and crushed her to him."Emily, these are different times now. The days of leaving doors open are over. The days of trusting strangers are over. Now that I've found you, I promise not to let anything bad happen to you. Ever."

"Oh Pat. I'm touched by what you say but I'm not a delicate flower. I'll be careful." Of what, she didn't know.

"Please let me call a friend of mine. Pete O'Malley. He'll change the locks, put the best ones on-dead bolts-chains-peepholes, whatever I order, and he'll do it while I'm away." She shook her head."Do it for me then. For my peace of mind."

Pat lifted her chin. She saw the intense look in his eyes as he kissed all objections away. A few minutes later, his motorcycle roared into the night. Emily hoped it didn't wake the neighbors.

She rolled over and slept.

The next morning, Monday already? Whatever happened to Sunday? She blushed at that thought. Coffee pot plugged in, toast down, apple cut up, vitamins in a row; she needed them today after the geriatric gymnastics of the day before. With Patrick out of sight, Emily had misgivings about her behavior. Was she a slut, sleeping with this guy so soon? What happened to all the love she had for Larry? Was there room for a beginning with another man? Plagued with doubts, at the same time she felt so alive. A paradox. But she didn't feel lonely anymore and he talked as if they had a future.

She nibbled at breakfast while making notes. No school today so she didn't have to rush. It helped to write thoughts down and use them for reference.

1. Pat is a take-charge guy.

2. Easy to fall into old patterns with him.

3. Make sure he doesn't take charge of me. He has the dynamics to inhale a little woman like me. Don't disappear just as I'm getting ready to emerge.

4. Goals: learn computer skills

5. Do not lose sight of the above but if I do momentarily, be forgiving—old habits are hard to break. Two steps forward, maybe one step back for a while.

Emily read and reread the list. Her own plan.

Security locks made sense. That was Patrick's idea. Go with it. If Pete O'Malley called, the job was his but it was her expense not Pat's. No way. The phone rang. Pat, a man of his word, did not waste time. Larry had such a laid back personality, tomorrow was good enough or next week. Not this new man. Oh no. Well she grinned, it's a challenge.

As promised, Pat called every day at different times; morning, afternoon, night, she never knew when. She wondered if it was a subtle way of checking up on her whereabouts. Emily enjoyed the chats, the heavy breathing when they recalled their night of intimacy, although she didn't wait by the phone praying for a call. They made a date for his return Saturday night. When she hung up, her pulse raced in anticipation. Today was Thursday. What'll I put on? The question is what'll I take off? Oh Lordy. Too much fun.

After Mr. O'Malley installed the locks followed by a short safety lecture and a few Irish jokes, she paid him against many 'no you don't' and 'Pat won't be happy'.

The bedroom was scented with sex and vanilla candles burned low. Their bodies intermingled, contented and satiated. Emily played with his chest hair, a finger circled around his nipples.

"Keep doing what you're doing and I'll be ready again." She had the ability to thrill him. Emily, the seductress, drunk with power."Pat, I feel like we both got a great deal on a used car. What do you think about that?"

Pat pulled her close to him."I love you, Emily." The L word. He said the L word. And he didn't ask her to say she loved him.

"Do you want to know how I feel about you?" she said.

"Only if you want to tell me. Do you realize that we met two weeks ago?" A lazy half smile from Pat."I was Larry's girlfriend for five years before we were intimate and that was after the wedding."

He stretched a hand out to brush away strands of hair that had fallen over her face. She sat up suddenly, grabbed a corner of the blanket to cover herself, and moved away from him.

"I meet you, we say hello and wham, and we're in bed. Repeatedly."

"What are you saying, Emily?" His erection faded.

"That's not like me. I've always been cautious about choosing friends, about allowing people to get close, and look at me. I'm naked —"

"I can see that." The smile frozen in place,

"— with a man I just met and I don't know what it means?"

"What do you want it to mean?"

She lay down next to him and sighed. The candle flame sputtered and died. A thin trail of smoke rose up and disappeared.

"I guess it means I love you too." There. It was out in the open.

He exhaled breath he didn't know he was holding, the wall of hidden emotions gave way to tears. His face dug into the pillow.

Emily was astonished. Tough, in-control Pat cried."What is it?" She ran hands down his back, smoothed his hair.

"You love me. Words I prayed for and you said them. Thank you, Emily. I'm the happiest I've ever been because of you."

He turned over, they held each other, she felt him relax and doze. What a huge responsibility this love business. She never dreamed relationships were so complicated. She wanted him to be happy and thought they could have a good life together. One step at a time, old girl. You're not alone anymore. The L word has spoken.

Emily woke up first, in a talkative mood. Their relationship had reached a new plateau. At close-to-sixty who had time for a long courtship? She might have preferred another week or two, a month even, but at this pace there was no stopping Pat.

"Let's do lots of stuff together." She poked him to wake up.

"We already do," he mumbled, half asleep.

"Not just running and taking off all our clothes, you goof."

"What's the matter with that? I thought you loved running and getting naked as much as I do."

"I do, but there's other stuff we can do together with our clothes on."

"Oh yeah? Like what?" He groaned. She was too energetic for him at the moment. He needed strong coffee to jump start his heart in the morning, let alone have an animated conversation.

"Like join the swim team," she announced in a strong tone that rang an alert."I love competition."

"I don't have time, not now—"

"Not to worry, this is a future plan. As long as you promise." she ran fingers down his chest, he watched them disappear under the blanket.

He grabbed her hand, held it still and ran the other hand through sleep tossed hair, resigned to the fact that she was up, therefore he had to wake up, and it began to feel as though the rest of him was already up.

"Ms. Emily?"

"Hmmm?"

"I do love waking up with you."

35

She gave him the big Emily smile."So where were we?"

"Hey, don't stop."

All innocence."But we were in the middle of a serious discussion and I—"

Warm skin, not fresh from a shower but okay for now, one leg, then the other, as he maneuvered into position, smooth talking all the while, "Okay, I'll join the swim team when I can if you agree to learn martial arts. Next to being with you," he slid inside her moist center eager for him,"inside of you," he lifted up, then down,"that's one of my favorite things." Up and now deeper.

Breathless, said,"What?" What the hell was he talking about? She'd ask later.

Later Emily said,"What?"

"Martial arts. It's great for balance, health, harmony and protection."

"I can't do that."

"Of course you can. You do it every day in running. This is more and even better. I learned as a young kid. Is that a deal?"

She had to think it over. Did she really want to learn how or would she revert to the old habit of capitulation to keep the peace? She was an expert at that.

Emily wasn't surprised to hear her voice say,"Okay. It's a deal."

You're biting off more than you can chew this time. Two steps forward. One step back.

"Deal."

Emily knew she had a satisfied man.

Chapter 10

Preoccupied with the sexual haze she was in, Emily hadn't told her daughter about the new man in her life. This time Emily had so much to tell but not to Meg. Not to anyone, except maybe Lola, her only single friend. A careful editing was called for. Meg encouraged her mother to go out, have fun but not this much fun.

In the midst of polishing the dining room table, why was she doing such a homely chore—who cared if the table had a shine to it?—the phone rang. She picked up the portable and continued her task. The wood was old and soaked up the polish.

"Mom," Meg's worried voice said,"I haven't talked to you all week. Even longer. Where've you been? Are you okay?"

"Yes, dear, I'm more than okay. I met a very nice man at the uh, club membership party and I've seen quite a lot of him since." Saw him with and without his clothes more than once, oh yes. Her face flushed with thoughts of how exciting this romance was.

Good thing Meg wasn't there to get a good look at her. She'd guess in a minute what her mother was up to. Funny how kids think their parents are asexual. Do they really believe that once parents conceive them, they never have sex again?

"Mom, please be very careful with this man. I want to meet him before you go any further. Do you know what I mean?"

Emily smothered a laugh."I hear you, honey. Thanks for your concern, but remember I am a grown up lady and I have good taste. After all, I married your Dad. And of course I want you and Jake to meet him soon. He'll be traveling for a couple of weeks but we'll get together."

"Okay, Mom. I'm going to call Tom. We worry about you all the time. Tom calls at least once a week from wherever he happens to be... He says, in that big brother deep voice he uses with me, it's my job to keep an eye on you. That puts a lot of pressure on me, Mom." No matter how old kids get, they still whine about each other, telling tales to Mom. It never ends, thought Emily."Tom will want to meet this guy, too," she continued."What's his name?"

"Patrick Corwin. He's a lawyer and a runner."

Emily laughed as she listened to her daughter, now a teacher at The School for Hearing. Parents trusted her to watch over their kids. She pictured Meg and Tom with their heads together, up to no good when they were little. Now she was married to a sweet young man Jake, in his own contracting business, and Tom had recently married Julie, but brother and sister remained close.

"You'll like Patrick a lot. I'll call tomorrow and we'll make a plan. 'Bye, honey."

"Wait Mom. I forgot to ask about the computer. Did you take it out of the box yet? Did you sign up for a class?"

"I signed up for Introduction to Computers. First class is tonight. Gotta run"

"Great. Bye, Mom. Love you."

"Love you, too."

She didn't mention the letter from Mark Wagner received today. Too late for you, Mark. Her heartbeat quickened when she saw the letterhead, the familiar watermarked linen stationery Mark and Sally used for years, an embossed gold C at the top. His handwriting was perfect, each letter formed according to the cursive writing book.

"Dear Emily, I hope you can forgive this old friend for poor behavior these past months. I have been wallowing in depression for our losses and am just coming out of it. Please say yes to dinner or lunch or whatever as long as we have a bit of private time. Call me. I promise to return your call. Mark"

She would call and meet with him but their opportunity for more than that was over now that Pat was in the picture, in her bed.

A couple of swipes with the polish cloth and the table sparkled from her effort. Lemon fragrance clung to her skin reminding Emily of all the years of role as the nurturer, the homemaker, a job she used to revel in. The smile faded when she caught her reflection in the table. She looked like Wifey. What became of the resolution to take charge of her life, not to depend on a guy?

Yet here she was with another strong man, even stronger than her husband and for a moment she almost forgot plans to grow up. Take small steps and don't lose yourself. She threw the cloth across the floor and ran upstairs to change. Emily Kendrick was going to school.

Chapter 11

Emily drove through town toward the college where she taught. A comfortable feeling. Before raising the car window, she inhaled a deep breath of warm Spring air. 6:30 p.m., still light out, what a pleasure after the darker nights of northern Florida in the winter. Not so chilly since after meeting Pat a few weeks ago, she thought and smiled. Hot as a matter of fact.

She could have parked in faculty parking but this seemed closer to Computer Science. Physical Education section was her domain. Kids careened around the parking lot in a frantic search for an elusive space. In an unaccustomed aggressive move, Emily beat someone into place and the guy gave her the finger. She jumped out, slammed the car door and yelled at him. "You're rude, Mister. Would you like someone doing that to your mother?"

He backed up the electric blue convertible until he was close enough to touch and looked her up and down, an insolent grin on his adolescent face. "Nice move, Lady. Nobody beats me out in the parking lot. You new here?"

Times sure have changed, she thought. "I am not talking to you until you apologize. That was disgusting." Emily retrieved her handbag, bottled water, and spiral notebook purchased for the class, and turned toward the maze of buildings, mystified as to what direction to take. She didn't know this part of the campus. "Where is," she consulted the admission sheet, "Academic 1?"

He laughed. "Thought you weren't going to talk to me—"

"Come on. Help me out here. I don't want to be late."

"Okay." He pointed straight ahead. "Stay to the right. The first building is #1."

Calling thanks over her shoulder as she ran, she said, "You still owe me an apology."

"I'll walk you to your car after class, okay? Sorry about the finger thing."

The path was crowded with kids; baseball caps worn backwards, jackets open, girls with belly buttons on display—didn't they know it looked ridiculous and indecent—this wasn't the beach for God's sake—guys in stupid ill-fitting pants. In the distance, Emily spied some gray heads and hurried to catch up.

Breathless she said, "Computers?"

"Walk this way," they said and chuckled. They were both using walkers.

Emily admired their sense of humor. Her problems were small by comparison. Into a red brick building they went, followed signs to the room number, entered and sat in the few remaining seats. At a glance, Emily counted about twenty five people, all adults, and a lot of gray hair. The big clock showed seven.

School. Emily couldn't believe it. The desks were larger than she remembered but they had to be to accommodate the soon-not-to-be dreaded computers. As a physical education teacher, she was in the gym most of the time. So few desks were needed, ever. The smell was different. Gone the scent of erasers and chalk. Right. Gone with the horse and buggy. She bet all her fellow students remembered the smell of chalk.

An impossibly young man stood behind a computer desk facing the class. He slid small glasses up the bridge of his nose and began talking rapidly and too soft for Emily to hear. All she made out was his name, Leonard something. After that nothing. She raised her hand. He ignored her. She called out.

"Leonard. I'm Emily Kendrick. I don't know about the rest of the class but I can't follow what you're saying." She spoke slowly and louder than usual in order for her voice to carry to the back of the room. "Does anyone agree with me?" A bunch of nods and yes's from the class.

He looked around, shrugged his shoulders and started again. This time his voice was stronger and slower. The class rewarded him with applause. He grinned, pleased with himself, and began a lecture on the history of computers and how they worked.

Emily fidgeted for a few minutes. She wondered if anyone else was bored. One woman doodled on a notebook; another student seemed to be balancing a checkbook... Her generation was too polite in the face of authority, in this case, a young teacher. Since no one objected to the subject matter, she decided to speak up again. "Excuse me."

Startled by the interruption, he acknowledged her. "Yes?"

"I don't know about the rest of the class, but I enrolled to learn how to turn on the computer, how to send e mail and use the Internet.

History and how it works doesn't hold interest for me right now. I'm getting older by the minute and I can't wait to begin using this contraption without being afraid of it."

To Emily's surprise and Leonard's consternation, the group applauded. They agreed with her.

"Okay kids," he began again, a smattering of laughter from the class, "who knows what a desktop is?"

Everyone was puzzled by what appeared to be a dumb question. A few of the seniors hit the tops of the desks in response.

"Hey," said the man with the walker, "Don't you make fun of us. Someday our grandkids will be making fun of you."

Leonard apologized. "You're right. I'm sorry."

His attitude changed as he had them 'boot up' and there was the desktop display. From then on, instruction was to the point, questions flew, gnarled fingers played hunt and peck at keys and two hours went by in a flash. The next class was in two days and the assignment was to get a good Internet connection and an Email address.

Seniors zipped up jackets helping each other when needed as they headed out of the building into the chilly night air. Some of them stopped to point out the brilliance of stars in the cloudless sky. Tall light poles showed the way to the parking lot. Emily ran back to the room for her water bottle and was last to leave. She flung open the door, looking for someone to walk with and bumped into the young man from the parking lot. The one who gave her the finger. The bottle went flying. He scrambled after it. The same grin was on his face as he used his jacket to wipe the bottle. He was much younger than she thought at first glance.

"You. What are you doing here? Aren't you a bit young to be in college?"

"No thanks?" he said, cheeks flushed red with embarrassment.

"No sorry?" she said. "Thanks for the water."

"Sorry for the bird. Sometimes I feel like I have to act tough. Dumb."

They laughed.

"This is silly. Really, what are you doing here and pardon me for being nosy but how old are you?"

He ignored the question. "Finished class, ran over to walk you to your car. In case you didn't notice, it's dark outside. If you were my mom, I'd want someone to watch out for you."

Emily felt a rush of pleasure from the young man. "You remind me of my son, Tom. He's older than you, a lot older, but this is something he'd do. What are you, fifteen, sixteen?"

She couldn't wait to tell Pat about this kid when he called later from wherever he was. "I'm Emily Kendrick. I'm the track coach here."

"Erle Lim. Friends call me the Geek as in computer geek." He paused, made a quick decision by the look on his hairless face. "Promise not to tell anyone—" and waited as she gave the Girl Scout salute. "Sixteen. I'm almost through with high school and I get my associate degree here next month and then I have a full scholarship to UCLA." He came up for air.

"Yeah. An over-achiever. Now I have to hurry home because I don't have my senior drivers' license and driving after nine is a no-no."

They walked down the path, chatting as if they'd known each other for a long time.

Erle asked her what she learned in class and Emily told him about the homework assignment.

"My computer is still in a dust covered unopened box. After two hours with Brian, I have a vague idea of how to get started."

Keys in hand, Emily approached her car. Erle said, "When's your next class?"

"Two days."

"I can come over after school tomorrow. Take me about thirty minutes to set up."

She dropped her stuff in the car. "Really? You'd do that for me?"

"No sweat. Where is your son right now?"

She had to think for a minute. "Upstate New York. Why?"

"He's not around to help you, so I will. Someday, if I'm out of town and my mom needs help she can call him. Deal?"

She hugged him. "Deal. You are a sweetie, Erle." Emily wrote her phone number and address on paper from the spiral notebook, ripped it out and gave it to him. "I'll have milk and cookies ready for you. Three o'clock good?"

"More like four. Chocolate chip, please."

Emily drove off. Her life was on track with a new man in her life, a new skill to be learned, in control with one step at a time.

Coming home wasn't as traumatic as it had been before meeting Pat. Comfortable in bed after a hot shower, a romance novel next to the lamp, Emily settled in and hoped Pat called before she fell asleep. The phone rang as she placed a marker in the book. A now familiar heat rose in her center in anticipation of hearing his deep voice. "Hi. I was about to turn out the lights."

"Hello my love. How was your day? Did you do anything special today?"

"Yes, as a matter of fact. I started school." Emily giggled. Sometimes he made her feel as if she were a little girl.

"School?"

She realized he had forgotten she was enrolled in a computer class. Well, why not, she rationalized. It wasn't important to him that she expand her skills. His business was much more important. She wouldn't make an issue of it. "Computer class. It started tonight and it was terrific and the best thing about it was that I met a young kid who's coming over tomorrow to set up my computer. He'll hook me up with the Internet and Email and..."

Pat broke in. "Don't let a stranger in your home while you're alone."

"Calm down, Pat." Heat had flown replaced with explanation. "He's a computer whiz who offered help and I accepted. Case closed, counselor."

"What does he expect from you in return for his generous offer of help, dear Emily?" Sarcasm dripped from every word.

She didn't like him right now.

"Chocolate chip cookies and milk. He's sixteen. I don't think he shaves yet. And I don't like you telling me what to do."

"Sorry. My experience is that you shouldn't trust anyone. Let's talk about the martial arts class sooner than later. I'll be home Friday night. I love you." He hung up.

So much for an easy relationship. Emily hit the light and shut her eyes. After the peculiar conversation, sleep was elusive. She didn't even know where Pat was calling from and yet he wanted to know every little thing she did. Why? What was the big deal?

Four o'clock the next day, the doorbell rang. As promised,

Erle Lim was at the door, stuffed backpack slung over a shoulder. Straight black hair mussed by strong wind, he wore a pressed white shirt with a tie and neat chino pants. A big grin creased his face as Emily opened the door.

"Come on in and don't you look nice. Did you have an interview or something special today?"

"You're what's special, Ms. Emily. And this is a business call." He swaggered in, sniffed the air like a puppy when he caught the chocolate scent, played it cool as he looked for the computer. She directed him to the small office next to the kitchen.

Emily knew she was in the presence of a young Alpha male. She had cleared what used to be Larry's catch-all desk and polished the top. Again with the polish. There was room for the computer on the gleaming surface, a printer filled with copier paper in the tray, a phone, assorted pens, pencils, and note pads. Everything she'd need for whatever she chose to do. At this point, she didn't have a clue.

"Nice. I like how you arranged stuff," he said as busy hands rearranged the desk. "To work." Bag on floor, leg flung over a chair, he was at home.

She dragged a kitchen chair in and sat behind him. "Mind if I watch?"

He grunted as fingers flew, pictures appeared on the screen, desktop info showed up.

"You like munchkins?"

"What?" Emily watched, fascinated as a parade of munchkins from the Wizard of Oz decorated the screen. "What is that?"

"Screensaver. You like?"

"Well, okay. It's funny. I always say, if it makes you laugh, keep it."

"Cool." Erle clicked a few more times and grabbed the phone. Using an authoritative deep voice, he spoke to someone and over his shoulder said, "Pick a user name and a password. First name that comes to mind. Don't censor yourself."

"Emily. That's a user name. And uh, runners. Password." Her cheeks warmed from excitement and the pressure of keeping up with this whirlwind. "Did I do good?"

"Call waiting. Do you want it?"

"Like on the phone?"

"Yeah, but instead of the phone ringing forever when you're on the Internet, a screen pops up and tells you who's calling. You want it?"

Emily thought for a second. She didn't want to spend extra money. "Is it extra dollars?"

"No. Trust me, Ms. Emily. It's cool." He hung up the phone, stood up, stretched and straightened his tie. "Your turn." He gestured to the chair. "You sit, take notes, hands on the computer, and then it's chocolate chip cookies and milk for the teacher. I have a seven o'clock class at the college."

By five, Emily's head was spinning but she knew enough to get on the Net, to send Email, and the notes would see her through. "I give up. Show me how to shut down with breaking anything."

A few minutes later, she smiled as Erle bit into cookies she baked that morning. The sight took her back to earlier happy times when young children who looked like combinations of she and Larry sat at that very table. Pat's phone conversation the night before invaded the pleasant daydream.

Erle ate another cookie and drank some milk. The back of his hand served as a napkin and he wiped away crumbs.

"Do you know anything about martial arts? My friend wants me to learn so I can protect myself."

Erle finished the last cookie, drained the milk glass, and carried the plate and glass to the sink. "Smart guy. I agree with him. Everyone in my family has been a student of the art since forever. There's a Dojo about ten miles south of St. Augustine. The Sensei is the best. He's a Master."

"Oh." Emily rose and followed him to the sink. He used a soapy sponge to wash the utensils.

"Yeah. I tell my mom all the time not to let anyone come in that she doesn't know. She's a black belt." He wiped his hands on a towel, grabbed his bag, and headed for the door. "Call me if you run into a snag but I think you'll do fine." He kissed her cheek and ran down the front steps. "See you on campus, lady, or maybe at the Dojo. That means school. Sensei means teacher."

Emily leaned against the closed front door. What a kid. She thought about what he'd said and realized it was time to trust her instincts. To let common sense guide her. She didn't need Pat or anyone else to caution her. When she taught her youngsters to look both ways before they crossed the street, and not to talk to strangers, she trusted them to do just that. She let go of them. Now she must let go of herself. Martial arts might be just the thing for her. She straightened up and marched over to the computer, gave it a loving pat and turned her thoughts to dinner. What was she in the mood for tonight?

The phone rang as she snooped through the refrigerator.

"Where have you been?" said Lola. "I've called you at all hours and no Emily to be found. And what are you eating?"

"Nothing yet. Foraging through pitiful leftovers." She pulled out a three day old carton of chicken and broccoli. "How long does Chinese food keep in the fridge?" Without waiting for an answer, she popped it in the microwave.

"You sound different, Emily. Moist, a state I am familiar with, not at the moment sorry to say, but you definitely sound moist."

"Are you a detective as well as one of the foremost portrait artists in the country?" Emily giggled. "Well Lola, I'm in lust with an option for love."

"Emily, my little virgin queen. I must tell you that I am shocked to hear you talk like this."

Removing the over-heated food from the microwave, she uncovered the container letting the steam escape. She slumped in a chair, appetite gone along with the excitement of telling Lola. "Virgin queen? What does that mean?"

After a lengthy pause, Lola said, "In my mind, ever since we met and swapped life's stories, I have always thought of you as a virgin." When Emily tried to interrupt, Lola cut her off. "Just listen, please. You were a virgin when you married Larry at what?"

"Twenty."

"Twenty. Right. Thirty faithful years. One man. To me, that's as close to a virgin as you can get. And now you tell me you just met someone and you are about to have sex—wait a minute, are you saying you already had sex with someone you just met?"

"Yes, I am definitely having sex with someone I first met on the beach and then at the swim club's membership party. I see him just about every day and night when he's not on the road, and I feel like a kid again. And foolish me, I thought you would be happy. You're the one who said get out and meet people so I did." She shut up, not wanting to beg for approval. This conversation wasn't going well at all.

When Jeanine spoke she was cool, distant. She said she was busy, new client appointment and all."I must run, darling. Talk to you soon." And hung up.

So much for having a friend share the happy news. She felt on edge the rest of the evening but shifted her unease to the back burner. Girlfriends. Bah humbug. Dickens was right. Being with Patrick felt too wonderful to be wrong. In a few days, he was coming home to her, to her bed.

Chapter 12

Emily could not remember a time like this in all her life except when she was a kid and her worst enemy was the mirror. All she seemed to be doing lately was dressing, undressing—thank you, Pat—working with the team who had reached the semi-finals in the state competition, getting used to her laptop and running.

This time the occasion was not one she looked forward to. A few weeks ago, she'd have given up chocolate forever to be with Mark Wagner. Not anymore. They had a date for lunch, one he requested in the letter she received and she had to tell him about Patrick. She had to. Two young couples always together, hot summer days skipping stones across the river, nights confiding inner thoughts as they sat by the fire. The girls were brought up to value virginity, to save the ultimate closeness for the man you married. The boys learned enough about sex on their own to keep them happy while they waited for the wedding vows. An innocent time.

Emily and Mark used to be best friends. They knew everything there was to know about each other. Mark was faithful to Sally as far as she knew, just as she was all the years with Larry. There were a few times when they were thrown together, alone in Mark's kitchen once when Sally was away, in a cabin on vacation for a short while, temptation was there but they resisted. Too late now. She felt frustrated, cheated somehow. This was bad. And she looked great today. Sex agreed with her. Eyes sparkled, skin glowed. Would he guess? No. He would think she looked wonderful and be ready to make his move. Oh, Mark.

Backing out of the garage, she turned on the radio and the windshield wipers in time to hear the weather report."It's another beautiful afternoon in St. Augustine." Emily stopped the car and looked through the windows. Why had she thought it was raining? Because it's raining inside of you. It's a blizzard of feeling. Put on your boots and slog your way through. Sure.

As Emily parked at the O'Hara's south on the beach, Mark pulled in next to her. And he looked marvelous, hair a touch more gray at the temples, men got away with that. Impeccable in a beige linen jacket, brown trousers, white shirt and tie, brown boots. She had an urge to muss his perfect hair and restrained herself. Ever the gentleman, he opened the car door but to her surprise he pulled her into his arms. The kiss was soft, yet powerful like everything about Mark. He didn't have to shout to get what he wanted. Body heat swept through her and she was forced to break the kiss.

"Hi." Deep breaths and slow down. "I've missed you," she said and knew any chance of a life with Mark was about to end.

He held her at arm's length for a minute, smiled and guided her up the wide plank steps.

Bowing and scraping preceded them as they were escorted to a window seat over-looking the ocean. Without a word from Mark, Chardonnay was poured into crystal stemware and salads appeared. Obviously, the esteemed professor of law at the University of Jacksonville was a respected patron of the fine establishment.

"I'm impressed, Mark. I've never been here before but you have. Clients? Dates?"

"Clients, Emily. I haven't gone out with anyone since Sally died last year." He searched her face for a hint of what was on her mind. "Now, let's catch up. It's taken me a long time to be alone with you."

Too long, Mark.

"If you can picture me on a couch, I consulted with a therapist after Sally died. It's taken all these months to face my feelings." He removed his glasses, cleaned them and gave her 'the ball's in your court look'. "Tell me what you've been doing. Work is all I do. Not worth talking about."

Emily gulped some wine. So soon. She thought a segue into her activities might be possible but—

"Let's see. I started college." She smiled, another sip, big sip of wine.

"Tell me about it. What are you taking and why?"

"Introduction to Computers. Overdue. The kids gave me a laptop. My track team is in the state semi finals this year. And I'm about to learn martial arts." She tasted a miniscule bite of lettuce.

"That's interesting."

And so it went until somehow Emily finished the wine and almost the salad and she felt woozy, unaccustomed to drinking in the afternoon with a dark secret that needed spilling.

Mark picked up on the fact that something was amiss and reached for both her hands. "Talk to me, Emily. Don't eat anymore and don't drink." He beckoned a waiter and ordered coffee the way she liked it, decaf black with a sweetener. "Speak to me."

Tears trickled down, twin streaks through makeup carefully applied an hour before. "Sorry," she sniffled. "I love you, Mark. You know that. I have for years. I thought we had a future and when you didn't return my calls, I figured I was way off base and a month ago," more tears, "I met someone and we've been —you know—" she couldn't look at him, "intimate and I know how important it always was for all of us to be chaste and well, virginal faithful like old-fashioned values but I had to tell you and," she looked up.

Mark was standing, a look of unbearable sadness on his face. Wallet in hand, money on table, he leaned over and kissed the top of her head, whispered that it was his fault, he would always love her and be there if she needed him and he was gone.

Stunned, she sat alone facing the view of the ocean and blotted tears until they stopped. Did she have to tell the truth and hurt both of them, ruin what might have been? She thought Mark didn't feel about her the way she felt for him so she moved on. That was okay. Of course it was. Stop beating yourself up. Now he was ready to make a commitment and she had to tell him about Patrick. Give it a rest. Go home. Get a life.

Emily opened her handbag, removed a mirror and tried to take a look at herself. Cursing softly she rummaged some more, found reading glasses and slipped them on. There she was—too old for all this soul searching—like daytime drama. Tune in tomorrow, folks. Can this middle years widow continue having sex with this interesting widower? Will they marry and live happily ever after? She couldn't wait to find out.

Emily straightened her shoulders, stood up, held on to the table before she took the next step and the next step. Nothing like crying in public to sober you up, she thought, and drove home.

Chapter 13

Tired of his hidden perch, disgusted with glass fragments scattered at his feet from expensive binoculars broken in fits of anger, Clifford Lansdale rose up and stretched. Back aching, out of meds, he went inside the palatial mansion to phone his lawyer. Patrick Corwin had been unreachable for a week. Out of the country on business. What more important business could he have than my case, he thought. Yet young Pat's the one guaranteed to get him out of this mess. Money spread around and all would be forgotten. Some called his investment plans greedy and said he stole millions. What fools. Patrick Corwin would make it all go away and then he, Clifford Lansdale would make Patrick Corwin go away. For good. The Goddess would soon be his.

First, he needed a new prescription filled and immediately. Second, the lawyer must pay a house call.

The New York doctor phoned in a prescription to the local St. Augustine pharmacy.

"Hello, Patrick. You've been incommunicado. I don't appreciate that. Make time this morning. I don't care. Be here at noon. And pick up my prescription at Dobbs Pharmacy down at the corner as you make the turn to my home." He banged the phone down. Liked the sound so much he lifted and banged it again.

The Dojo was a wooden structure nestled small among palm trees, palmettos, cactus babies growing wild in the sand and saw grass surrounded by oriental gardens. Nervous, Emily entered with Patrick and a gym bag but she presented a picture of calm as she met the Sensei. A helper gave her a white ge, the uniform, and white belt and showed her to the locker room. Patrick took a seat and waited. An air of formality was practiced, a protocol, and Emily liked it right away. A few much younger women were also in the locker room and everyone chatted. Emily was the oldest and called the new guy.

Starting Over

The first class was devoted to conditioning, stretching, stances and blocks. A lot of the movements were familiar to Emily but the discipline was far different than anything she'd ever experienced. After an hour, the class bowed to the Sensei and it was over. Emily couldn't wait for the next class. Two or three times a week would put her in great shape with a good understanding of what to do if attacked. So said Patrick on the way back to St. Augustine where they'd agreed to go the club. He was entered in a swim competition and Emily could relax and visit with her friends.

On the way, Pat told her a little about his strange demanding client and the errand to pick up a prescription nearby. Because of client confidentiality, he couldn't say much more except that he was sorry to have accepted the case. Emily forgot about it when they reached the club.

Shelly sidled over and appraised her old friend. "Emily, your complexion glows. It's obvious to me your boyfriend treats you very well."

"My boyfriend? We're many decades beyond that title." She enjoyed watching their faces as they saw her in a different role. "He's my lover."

"Is this our Emily talking like the heroine of a romance novel?" Jesse said.

Emily grinned and turned around to find Margaret.

"As Shelly says, nice very nice," Margaret said in a deep phony southern accent. Margaret grew up in New Jersey. The women cracked up over the expression they'd used since forever.

"Will he join and become a new member?" Shelly said. The play on words was not lost on Emily. "Well, he is your new member, isn't he?"

"Enough already," said Emily and they howled with laughter.

Pat climbed out of the pool, a pleased expression on his face. He had won his first ten lap competition and was talking to the other men. She crooked a finger and he excused himself.

"My ball and chain beckons," he called over his shoulder.

"Your ball and chain?" She was incredulous. "Don't ever call me your ball and chain. That's archaic."

"But honey —"

"This may not be the right place but it's on my mind so here goes. I've given this serious thought.

"Is this a bad thing? I don't want to hear a bad thing."

She rummaged through the gym bag, found a small towel, and mopped his face, aware that her friends might be watching.

"I think it's a good thing. Would you like to live with me? We're compatible, more than compatible, and I miss you too much when we're not together."

Pat was speechless. "Give me a chance to catch my breath, you gorgeous, wonderful light of my life." He shook his head in disbelief. "Emily, you've made me an offer I can't refuse. I'll get to wake up next to you every day for the rest of my life."

"So the answer is yes?' Her face turned red from the look in his eyes.

"Of course. In fact, you're so delectable in your shorts, if we weren't with all these nice folks, there's another game we might play."

She hurried over to talk to her buddies.

"You didn't tell us you were living together," Jesse said after Emily told them Patrick was moving in.

"Almost. We'll try it. See if it works." She patted her shoulder." Don't worry, Jesse, I'll be fine."

Margaret said, "I'll be right back." She headed over to the bench where Pat was, still smiling.

"Where are you going?" Emily said.

Margaret ran back to the group. "I just wanted to see if there were scorch marks on the bench where you sat. I got kind of warm watching the two of you."

Emily shook her head and hugged her dear friends. "Be happy for me, okay?"

They chorused, "Okay." The afternoon was a success.

The merger, as they called it, began slowly. One Sunday he was invited to bring a business suit, stay overnight and go to work from her home. Until then, he had gone back to his condo on Sunday nights. This was a trial run to see how living together might work. Pat brought a suit and a jar of chunky peanut butter.

Emily laughed her head off at his priorities. She asked if he was worried she wouldn't provide him with the extra goodies he enjoyed. "No," he said. He noticed she liked creamy but he liked chunky. Like a little kid who packs his favorite teddy bear.

"Throw your soiled clothes in the washing machine. I'll do a wash tomorrow," she said. "That's a perk for being my boyfriend."

"Boyfriend? We're a bit old for the boyfriend-girlfriend routine."

"I didn't say it. Someone at the club called you my boyfriend. It made me laugh."

Early Monday morning, she prepared a breakfast of whole wheat pancakes with sliced strawberries and strong coffee. No team practice today and classes were later. Served on the deck overlooking the ocean, it was an idyllic setting. A lingering kiss with promise of more to come and he went off to work, a happy man.

The phone rang a minute later. "Does this mean I won't have to stop at Mickey Dee's for an egg Mac Muffin and coffee anymore?" Pat clicked off.

Emily watched his car disappear and thought about all the lonely mornings before they met. He was important to her, and in such a short time. Lucky me, lucky us.

She hummed 'Love is lovelier, the second time around', started a wash in motion, and then looked at the disarray left from the active weekend. Lots of athletic gear. And now the new white uniform called Ge. She hung up her white tie belt and vowed to make yellow belt before long.

She began a frenzy of organization, as if possessed with anger. She was entitled to happiness with someone other than her husband, she knew that. Larry was dead, she wasn't. If the situation were reversed, she'd have wished a full life for him. Get on with your life and get over misgivings that come up once in a while. You have your permission to be happy with Pat.

She transferred wet clothes to the dryer and there was Pat's underwear. The old sadness returned. It was an intimate chore, washing a man's clothes. A year ago her husband was alive. She had washed his clothes for nearly thirty years and believed they had at least forty more to go.

"Get a grip," she yelled. "This is twilight time. No more regrets." This dear man was in her life now and would be for the remainder of their years.

"Thanks, I needed that," she whispered.

Chores well under way, Emily checked to see if anyone

responded to her queries regarding travel work. Confidence in computer skills encouraged her to apply for a wide range of positions. "Yes," she shouted, new mail awaited her touch. An Email from Geek99@aol.com Erle Lim. She opened it. Hey lady, Greetings from Los Angeles. All is cool here. More to follow. Watch who you trust. CompCoach. She printed and filed it so she'd have a paper copy and sent a quick response. Her first 'puter buddy.

Chapter 14

By July 4th, Pat had moved out of the condo and the merger was complete. Tricky business, blending two lives but so far, so good. He traveled part of the time although mostly he was building a case for his important client. Under investigation, he said and shook his head. Sometimes he left for Europe or the Middle East and never said why. Their time together was precious, and each return brought renewed passion. Emily felt like a young bride.

Naked on the deck at night was a favorite pastime. The dunes and tall grass provided total privacy from neighbor's who would have been shocked at the wanton behavior of the widow next door.

Cicadas, playing their constant symphony, cloaked moans of delight in the dark. Clouds, in no hurry to reach a destination, prevented the moon from illuminating the deck. A light breeze, perfumed by summer roses, wafted over Emily and Patrick who luxuriated in a private world as they unraveled the mysteries of their bodies.

"It's time we did a bit of family blending, don't you think?" Emily said, one lazy summer night on the back deck. "Meg threatened to barge in unexpectedly, if she and Jake aren't invited immediately. She's had enough of my excuses."

Pat covered his nakedness with a towel, as if Meg might knock at the door any minute.

"She's right. I've heard similar words from my daughter. It's just that when I come home from a trip, the only place I want to be is inside you."

He rolled over and grabbed at empty space in the dark. His towel came off, pulled by her unseen hand.

Emily's voice whispered in his ear from the other side, "Darling, I hope you don't think I'm too forward —" her hand slid down his body and found the object of her desire, "but I've wondered what it's like to be the aggressor, and tonight's the night to find out."

His breathing grew ragged as she stroked him with a soft touch followed by gentle squeezes. A warm lotion spread by sure fingers and it didn't take long for his back to arch with passion. Her warm, wet mouth took him in.

"Emily, oh Emily, not so fast."

She didn't slow, didn't listen to him. She sucked and kissed him until he climaxed, and held him as he shuddered with pleasure. They snuggled under the big velvet towel.

Pat's voice was soft, deliberate, a caress to her ears. "I want us to be married."

The M word reared its lovely head.

She took a long time to respond. She'd thought about marriage, what it would be like, how it would feel to have his last name. To relinquish Larry's name, the name she'd carried most of her life. She was Pat's woman now, and he was her man. Were there any reasons not to be married? She couldn't think of one.

"Yes. I want us to be married too."

This was a meal to be digested. All was quiet on the deck except for the symphonic night bugs celebrating the good news.

Pat lifted her fingers to his mouth and kissed each one. "You won't regret this, dear. I promise to take care of you as long as I live."

"I guess it's time to bring our children together."

"I guess so."

A family gathering took place the following weekend. Tom and Julie drove in from their new home in Virginia and the girls were available. Fresh flowers adorned the inside and outside of the house. A barbecue was planned, all was in readiness. The children were coming.

"I'm a wreck," Emily told Jesse. "What if they don't like him? What if—I don't know."

"They'll like him. I do. Everyone at the club likes him. They might be resentful at first, somebody taking their Dad's place, but once they see how happy you are, they'll accept him, I'm sure."

"I hope you're right. Oops. The doorbell. How considerate. They didn't barge in. Pat's kept his clothes on all day just in case they arrived early. Bye."

When she ran down the stairs, a wonderful sight greeted

her. Pat poured on the charm as he shook hands with Tom and Jake and introduced himself to Meg and Julie.

"Hi kids," she said.

"Mom, you look beautiful," Meg said. She shook hands with Pat. "Looks like you two are doing well."

A cool greeting from Meg, thought Emily.

"We are," Pat said, his arm around their mother. "You and your Mom look alike. No denying where you came from. My daughter and her husband should be here soon. They're always the last to arrive. Come in. Make yourself at home." He stopped. "Sorry. This is the home you grew up in." An uneasy laugh from everyone.

Tom, in his deep manly voice said, "That's okay, Pat," the name not comfortable for him. "I can see Mom is pleased to be with you."

"Thanks, Tom."

"The grill is just about ready. I'll get the steaks on," Emily said.

"If it's all right with you, I'll tend to the meat," Tom said. He exchanged smiles with his sister. They knew from years of experience that their Mom was dangerous with the grill.

Choruses of "I'll make a salad," and "I'll set the table" and the kids took over the kitchen.

"What's going on, Emily?" Pat said. "Do they always take over?"

"Yes, dear. Nothing hostile. More like friendly fire. My reputation as a chef was ruined years ago." Emily laughed and led him to the deck. "Let them work while we relax with a glass of wine.

Amanda and Mike rang the doorbell to no avail. Laughter and music came from the house.

"They can't hear us." She tried the doorknob. "Come on. The door's unlocked."

Cautious, Mike said, "Are you sure it's okay to walk in?"

"Come on. My Dad lives here now."

They followed the sounds into the kitchen where Tom shouted orders to the others who chopped, sliced, and assembled a meal.

"Hi. This is the Kendrick household, right?" Amanda said.

"You must be the Amanda and Mike we've heard about," Tom said. "Grab the silverware and set the table. This is terrific, more people to boss."

Amanda and Mike shrugged their shoulders as if to say why not and dived into the family.

After dinner, Pat clinked a spoon against his water glass. "Attention please and a little respect for the grown-ups."

"Grown-ups, are there any grown-ups here?" said Tom. The kids cracked up.

"Hey," Amanda said, "that's my Dad."

The laughter was contagious. Even Pat smiled.

"Don't listen to them, dear. Give them a little food, they get silly. It happens all the time. They'll quiet down when you make our announcement."

Something important was about to happen. The kids simmered down and listened.

"We've decided to get married."

A moment for the news to sink in and then everyone applauded.

"Good news." Meg held her hand out to Amanda. "Welcome."

"I'm an only child. I've always wanted brothers and sisters."

"Cool. Seriously cool," said Tom, his arm around Julie who started to laugh. "What are you laughing about?"

"You all sound like The Brady Bunch meets Andy Hardy. I've been waiting for someone to say let's put on a show; my Mom can make costumes; we can use my Dad's barn. It's so normal, so wholesome. I love it."

Emily sensed something off with her daughter and decided to wait and see.

"Yeah, I like the sound of normal and wholesome. No one ever said that about us before," said Tom.

"Don't pay any attention to them, Amanda," Emily said. "By the way, you're all invited to the wedding." More laughter.

Emily brushed away a tear ready to spill. This was almost perfect. A new beginning. A new everything. She was ready. But first she went looking for Meg who had disappeared. Meg was curled up on the twin bed in her childhood bedroom, tears in her eyes.

Stroking her daughter's long hair so like her own, Emily said, "What's going on, honey? You're unhappy about something."

Meg cried harder. "Oh Mom. He'll take Dad's place and there won't be Dad here anymore. I hate him."

What to do, what to say? Show me the words, please. "Meg, sit up. And look at me. When you married Jake, you weren't replacing your father. You added to the family by getting married. Dad is gone but he lives in our hearts forever. You know that, don't you?" She nodded. "And your Dad wouldn't want me to be lonely without a companion. Pat is the one for me at this time in my life, honey. Now dry your eyes and come down."

"I'll try, Mom. That's all I can do."

Emily walked downstairs with her daughter and hoped Meg would get over it.

Later, when they were alone, Emily said, "What kind of a wedding should we have?"

Pat pulled a blank with the far-off stare men get. "Not too big, not too small."

"Thanks. Very good suggestions. Could you be a bit more specific?"

"I'll prop a ladder under the bedroom window, you'll climb down and we can elope."

"No. Bad idea. I'm afraid of heights. I'll fall off the ladder. How about a wedding at the club? When the tide is out and hurricane season has passed."

And so it went until they fell asleep in each other's arms, secure in the knowledge that a marriage was in the near future.

"Now that we're actually planning a wedding," Emily said, in bed the next morning, eyes still closed, "how about planning a honeymoon?"

"I've given that a lot of thought, my sweetheart. Would you care if I arrange a surprise honeymoon trip? There's a special place I have in mind."

Emily thought for a few minutes, eyes now open. They sparkled with excitement. "All right. As long as you reveal what kind of clothes are required."

"Pack swim suits, sunscreen, walking shoes, sandals, shorts, tee shirts, one long skirt, a shawl, a straw hat, two long dresses,

63

and your denim backpack. Your passport, too."

"This is very mysterious. How long can you get away from work?"

"Only one week."

"And you?"

"If we marry in September before school begins, I'm free for the trip. What about your client? Will the case be over before then?"

Pat scowled. "I hope to end the mess around that time."

"Okay, let's make plans for late August, early September. Now give me a clue as to where we're going."

Standing up, Pat flexed his muscles and made a move in Emily's direction. "I'll give you a clue and then don't ask me anymore. Deal?"

"Deal. What's the clue?"

"I want to make love to you as we travel through several time zones."

"What kind of a clue is that?" She smiled and giggled like a kid. This surprise idea aroused her. She was ready to make love in the Florida time zone.

His voice deepened as he reached for her. "I participate in a survey to study the effects of long distance travel on orgasms. This is my contribution to the study. Somebody has to do it. Since I'm a good citizen, I volunteered."

"What are you babbling about?" She looked at her husband-to-be. He tried to look serious but a smile tugged at the corners of his mouth and gave him away. The light bulb in her head clicked on.

"You're teasing me." She smacked his arm. "I'm so gullible."

"Yes dear Emily, you are. But, as long as orgasms are the topic of discussion—"

A yellow and white striped tent decorated with big pots of yellow and lavender chrysanthemums was set up on the patio of the swim club. The ocean shimmered with the reflection of the sun in the west; each guest was bathed in the soft light of evening. Emily was thrilled that the weather cooperated.

Lola came south from Jacksonville with her latest escort, a young hunk. Underwear model popped into Emily's mind. They hugged. "Sorry we haven't been in touch and thanks for the invitation. You will always be my virgin queen." Emily smacked her in the arm.

"Meet Pierre. His English is poor but his French more than makes up for it." Pierre kissed both their hands.

"Your gown is ivory silk, isn't it?"

"It is. I do feel like the virgin queen." They laughed a private laugh.

"It looks red in the sun's reflection. If I ever get married, may I borrow it?"

"Of course you can. It will be like new, worn only once. And Lola, I wish the same joy to you. You're so neat, you may borrow it to paint your next picture in, if you like."

Moving through the guests to find her groom, at the back edge of the gathering, she spied Mark Wagner. A knot formed in her stomach and she rushed to greet him but he was gone. Gone without saying hello, without wishing her well. She felt his pain. How different their lives would have been if only—would've, could've, should've. Emily searched the group for Pat and there he was, coming to take her hand.

They took their places before the Justice of the Peace. Everyone gathered around in a semi-circle as the couple exchanged vows. They spoke together. "Six months ago, we met on the beach. We met, fell in love, and we are starting over."

Pat said, "I promise to be your faithful husband. To care for you for the rest of my life."

Emily said, "You are in my heart forever. I promise this to you."

The JP declared, "By the power vested in me by the State of Florida, I declare Patrick Corwin and Emily Kendrick to be husband and wife; to love and cherish, in sickness and in health, for better or for worse, until death do you part."

A five piece band played the song "You Do Something To Me" by Cole Porter, a favorite with special meaning for the newlyweds. The family danced, everyone switching partners, and Meg kissed Pat on the cheek for the first time.

After the wedding festivities ended, the Corwin's were driven home. In the limousine, Patrick looked down at his wife, her head on his shoulder.

"You have a mischievous look on your face. What are you thinking about?"

She grinned. "What did Adam say to Eve in the Garden of Eden when he tiptoed up behind her and covered her eyes with his hands?"

"I don't have a clue."

"He said, 'Guess who'?" Emily laughed and couldn't stop.

When she realized Pat didn't share in her amusement, she said, "The image of the only two people in the world playing the silly game kids play always brings me pleasure."

Chapter 15

Behind binoculars, glittering eyes filled with malice. Black coffee dregs lay at the bottom of many broken cups on his hidden perch. An empty bottle of Vicodin needed a refill. His back throbbed with pain. Ah Clifford, old boy, now that Patrick Corwin's work is finished and you are off the hook, you can conjugate, what? No, concentrate on real justice. Lay off the coffee, Cliffy. He twisted the dial for a close-up. Zoom. Look at him with my Goddess.

Clifford Lansdale, cleared of charges by his young defense lawyer, shivered. And continued to shiver on this balmy September evening as the setting sun cast a glow changing the widow's walk to a deep red.

Chapter 16

Before they went on their honey moon, Pat insisted on having an alarm system installed, "It's an easy place to break into," he said.

Pat made sure the system would have kept the White House secure. Emily had to keep a straight face as he explained in great detail how to operate the system.

"Listen to me, so there won't be any false alarms sent. That's unacceptable. The security people who receive messages must have faith in us. We don't want to be known as the folks who cry wolf at the slightest sound."

"Will there be a written test after your explanation?"

Pained by her remark, he said, "This is all for you, for your protection. We live in a secluded area. When I'm not here, I want the comfort of knowing you're safe. The world has changed since we were kids."

Emily nodded as he spoke. She understood what he referred to.

"I'm sorry I was snippy. I didn't mean it. I remember the good old days when you never locked the car door or even the front door of your house. Please continue and when you're finished, I'm willing to take a test, written or oral."

Pat's eyes lit up and they smiled at each other.

"Okay, my star pupil. Notice the domes in the corners of the entrance hall. There are hidden cameras concealed behind them, on record all the time. If someone enters the house and the alarm isn't turned off in fifteen seconds, a silent alarm sounds at headquarters. They dial our home number to confirm. If it's an accidental alarm, we give them the code word and there's no emergency. Understand so far?"

"It's not rocket science. Of course I understand. Continue."

"Sorry, I got carried away." He took a few deep breaths to calm down. "Sometimes I get so intense, I scare myself."

"Relax please. I don't like it when you question my intelligence. One last time. You tell, I listen."

"Okay. The second alarm, with bells and whistles so to speak, goes off in the house in thirty seconds. You'll see flashing lights and a loud buzzing alarm will go off. The police are notified and a team of armed cops arrive with sirens blasting. The same happens if someone breaks into the back of the house."

Emily's eyes were huge as she took in all this information. Pretty scary stuff and Pat's fervent wish to protect her melted the misgivings she'd had about all the fuss. She pulled him close.

"Thanks my love. You've got the bases covered. I feel safe."

The next morning, Pat went for his daily five mile run. Emily ran earlier so she could try to finish packing. An hour later the doorbell rang. Annoyed by the interruption of packing for the mystery honeymoon, Emily hurried to the door and yelled, "Who's there?" She looked through the peephole. All that was visible were red roses, at least two dozen. Suddenly the roses dropped down to expose the face of her new husband.

"Guess who?" he said and opened the door, stepped into the foyer, and swept her in his arms. He covered her with thorn-less roses.

"Here I go again, crying because I'm so happy."

"My precious wife, I'll make sure that anytime you're moved to tears, it will be tears of joy."

A white stretch limousine arrived at noon. Emily, packed and ready to go on the mystery honeymoon, danced around the house. She couldn't stop moving from nervousness and excitement. The house was spotless but she always found one more task that had to be done. The nesting urge, some might call it. Like always wearing clean underwear in case you got in an accident. Of course Pat, ever organized with their bags at the door, watched his wife's antics with amusement.

When the doorbell rang, he hurried out, Emily and luggage in tow, loaded them into the limo, and ran back for a final check of windows, doors, and electrical appliances. Satisfied all was in order, he set the alarm, climbed in next to his wife, and the driver left for the airport.

Emily yelled, "Stop." The driver hit the brakes.

Pat said, "What's the matter? I did the final check. We have to hurry."

"Nothing serious, dear. I'll be right out." As she ran to the house, she heard Pat complain to the driver. "Women. Can't live with them, can't live without them." The men laughed. She didn't like that attitude, but what's a woman to do?

She disarmed the security alarm, hurried to her computer and sent a message to the widow's club she had joined months ago telling them she was fine, on her honeymoon and she'd be in touch when she returned. She didn't want anyone to worry. Then she reset the alarm system and ran back to the limo.

She knew Pat was annoyed. A pulse beat hard at his temple but she kissed him and said she was ready now. If it was business related, she would have been patient. Because it was something he considered trivial, he had no patience. He had a lot to learn. She was beginning to understand her needs were important too.

They proceeded north on I 95 and soon it was apparent Jacksonville Airport was the destination.

Pat signed for the ride, and told the driver, "Pick us up at four p.m. one week from today and thanks for good service."

"Have a great trip," the driver said. "My wife and I went to Israel two years ago. The best time we ever had." He drove off.

Emily was incredulous. "Israel?"

"He spilled the beans, but yes, Israel. I have an hour's worth of business in Jerusalem and wonderful plans for the rest of our time, at an exclusive resort at the beach in the southern tip of Israel. Are you disappointed?" He searched her face for any flicker of dissatisfaction. She was beaming.

"I've wanted to go there for years but it never happened. I wondered where you'd take us but never dreamed it would be to such an interesting country. I pictured a beach with palm trees, tango and cha-cha music, and piña coladas. And that would be fun, but Israel. I'm thrilled."

"For better or for worse, Emily, this is our first vacation. Be prepared for many heavily armed soldiers, suitcase and body checks before they let us into their country. Security is extremely tight." He looked serious for a moment. "There's something I have to tell you about myself and what happened years ago in Jerusalem where I have strong ties. I'll tell you about the story later."

"Okay." Emily thought she knew Patrick so well and there was something else to be revealed.

They entered the check-in line to wait their turn. Finally they boarded the plane and Pat's extra surprise was the first class accommodation.

"How else can I make love to you as promised?"

Emily went to the bathroom and removed her panties and bra. She wore a coral flared knit skirt, with a matching tee shirt, and long sleeved zippered jacket. Perfect for travel and fooling around. Already moist with excitement, she couldn't wait for the plane to take off. Her husband observed his wife as she swung her way down the aisle, on her face a special smile full of promise just for him.

He felt himself rise to the occasion as she brushed past to reach the window seat. Wine was served right away, followed by cheese and crackers, and the honeymoon began. Lights dimmed, the movie started and so did the Corwin's.

When the El Al flight ended twelve hours later, the satiated weary couple staggered out to be stopped and frisked several times before leaving the airport. Pat spied a driver with a card printed Corwin held high above his head.

"There's the driver who will take us to Jerusalem. It's only forty five minutes east. Maybe he'll speak English. My Hebrew is mediocre."

"Honey, if I'd known our destination, I'd have learned some basic Hebrew. I'm really quick with languages. Let's buy a phrase book and we'll get along fine. Besides, most people speak English wherever you travel."

"We don't need a guide book. I know enough to get by."

"Sorry dear, I must insist. Please ask the driver to stop where I can purchase such a book. Also, I want to learn rate of exchange, and most of all, I need to feel independent. Okay?"

Pat touched her face and nodded. "Okay. It's a good thing to learn."

The driver did speak a fractured sort of English and Emily took notes on places of special interest. The trip to Jerusalem wasn't scenic, mostly miles of barren sand. Then the city appeared on the horizon; rolling hills, ornate buildings, and as they drew closer, people in flowing robes, soldiers with ammunition belts, machine guns, grenades attached to their belts, and cell phones. Everyone had a cell phone in use.

Then they were in the city of Jerusalem, a mixture of old and new. The driver dropped them at the Arcadia Hotel, a bed and breakfast in the center of the great city. They'd be able to walk everywhere, except for the West Bank. Signs placed everywhere warned tourists to stay away.

Chapter 17

A tall, pencil slim, olive-skinned woman wearing a black silk jumpsuit cinched at the waist with a flowered red and black sash, greeted them. She smiled, flashed very white teeth with a bit of gold, and extended her hand.

"Shalom. Patrick Corwin, it is good to see you again." Pat kissed her on the cheek. "Mrs. Corwin, welcome to Israel. My name is Norith. After you register, Ben Ari will show you to your rooms and answer any questions you have about where to go and what not to miss. A repast will be brought to your room shortly."

Norith spoke in a precise English with almost no hint of an accent, as if she were educated in England. When asked later, she said, "Indeed, that assumption is correct."

Emily placed her left hand, gold wedding band on display, over Pat's right hand as he signed the register, Mr. and Mrs. Patrick Corwin, for the first time. She felt a glow emanate from deep inside. She had faith in her new husband, in their future together.

A handsome muscular man with shiny black hair, an embroidered yarmulke worn on the back of his head, picked up their bags and escorted them to their rooms. This was Ben Ari. He moved with a sensual grace, and hummed music the Corwin's were familiar with.

They exchanged looks as if to ask, do you know what he's humming?

They both shrugged and tried to recall the tune. Suddenly Emily started singing, "I Don't Get No Satisfaction" and Pat laughed out loud. Ben Ari turned, smiled, and nodded. "Rolling Stones," he said and continued to hum.

The sitting room was furnished with a small white couch for two, a chair and teak desk with writing accessories, a round table with two chairs, small refrigerator, and a television cabinet. A large Persian rug lay on the polished dark wood floor. Beautiful. Ben Ari left the bags at the door.

He said,"I shall return with a light repast."

"Do you like it? Will you be comfortable here?" Pat said.

"Like it? I love it and we've only been here 10 minutes. Let's check out the bedroom and bath."

"Okay, dear wife. Remember that Ben Ari will return very soon."

"Don't worry, dear husband. I won't take advantage of you."

"You won't?" She shook her head no. "Oh, I was hoping you would."

The bed dominated the spacious room. Everything was white; walls, doors, dresser, curtains, bedspread. The floor was inlaid tile with a Middle Eastern motif. The bathroom was the piece de resistance. Also white with the same tile, but in the center of the room was a sunken whirlpool big enough for two. The possibilities were endless. Emily wondered how much sightseeing they'd do with accommodations like this. Somehow they'd manage.

After a bottle of Israeli wine with crackers and soft white cheese, the new Corwin's decided to sightsee in the whirlpool. They found it to be a stimulating, cleansing event and promised to return soon.

Emily dressed in a red silk ankle length gown and red high heeled sandals, a red, white, and black flowered shawl over her shoulders to ward off the chilly autumn evening.

"You are lovely, my bride. Your hair is always streaked from the Florida sun," he lifted a strand.

Her dark eyes watched him as he gazed at her. The journey continued down her slim, youthful shape, and ended at toes seen through sheer stockings.

"You're everything and more than I've ever dreamed of."

Although they had been making love non-stop, Emily felt moist again.

Norith, at Pat's request, had reserved a table for them at a five star restaurant, Mishkenot. A taxi waited. Emily was surprised to see Pat haggle over the fare, but haggle he did and a price of twenty shekels was agreed on.

The drive seemed more like an amusement park ride as the driver careened through traffic, weaving and bobbing like a punch-drunk boxer. When he reached the destination, the driver hurried to open the door and assisted her to the curb. Pat thanked the driver and they bid each other Shalom.

Built like a lighthouse, tall and round, the restaurant was unique in appearance.

"Have you been here before?" Emily said.

"Many times, but it never fails to excite me. I'll tell you more over dinner."

To enter the restaurant, they first walked down a stairway, then up another stairway. An elegant gentleman, with the dark good looks Emily recognized as the 'Israeli' look, opened the multi-colored stained glass door as they approached. The men embraced.

"Shalom. Congratulations to you both. I am Samuel Levy, proud owner of Mishkenot. Thank you and your beautiful bride for honoring this establishment with your presence. A table by the window is waiting and champagne is already there. Compliments of the house. My best waiter will be at your service."

"Shalom, Samuel. It's good to see you once again. This is Emily, my bride of two days. I'm combining our honeymoon with a bit of business. I wanted her to have the pleasure of dining here."

She smiled at the formal informality of this exchange. It was obvious the men knew each other well, and this display was for her. Patrick was even more interesting than she imagined.

Samuel led them through several small dining areas, one more elegant than the other, each table occupied by well dressed patrons, a cacophony of languages blending in hushed tones. A table by the window was an understatement. Each of the three tables in the small dining room faced open French doors with a private balcony. When Emily turned to thank Samuel for the splendid table, he was gone. Pat shrugged. "It's his way, sweetheart."

Over a bottle of Dom Pérignon, Pat saw that his wife had questions she needed answers to. Their meeting six months before was a gale force whirlwind. Little time was spent on catching up with lives of longevity. They were both high mileage in years and it would take many more years of conversation and day-to-day togetherness to fill in the squares. This was a perfect time to learn more about each other.

"Samuel had one son. He, Yehuda, was my closest friend during the years I lived here. There was an incident at the West Bank. Yehuda saved my life. He lost his." Pat reached for her hand. "Emily, I owe this man a lifetime debt. Whatever he asks of me, I do. This restaurant is now one of the finest dining places in Israel, with the highest rating in travel guides. A success story in spite of his tragedy."

A slight cough was heard close by. They glanced up. The waiter stood like a sentry guarding the table. Menus were handed out with a flourish and the waiter left.

Emily's palate was in full arousal as she read the entrees. Succulent this, poached that, steamed and sauced, a gourmet paradise written in Hebrew, English, and French. Never adventurous when it came to dining out, Emily selected grilled salmon. Pat ordered Chateaubriand.

He had more on his mind. "We live in your home where you lived with your husband, sleep on the bed where you slept with him. Everything there is from your past life. I'd like us to start fresh. Not to move but to renovate. What do you say?"

"It never occurred to me. Well, now that I think about it, there have been times when I wished there weren't whispers of my former life around me." She sipped her drink. "Yes, Pat. That's a good plan. Jake's in construction. He can help us figure out changes. Our waiter has a huge tray and he's headed in our direction. Let's talk about this later. Much later."

After dinner, over tiny cups of espresso, Emily brought up the original question she asked when they first arrived at the restaurant.

"Why do you find this country so special?"

Pat's blue eyes darkened as he seemed to sort through many thoughts.

"Did I tell you that I was a Sociology major at the University of Minneapolis with a minor in Philosophy? All this before law school, of course."

Emily was surprised to learn about his education. "No, honey. We were too busy making love most of the time to share stories about college."

Lost in memories, he didn't hear her. "Part of me dwells on

man's inhumanity to man, crime and suitable punishment. Subjects like that. For instance, my father." Suddenly he gasped as if intense pain stopped him from speaking for a moment. His eyes closed and he struggled for composure.

Emily dipped a napkin in cold water and pressed it to his temple. "Pat," she whispered, "Pat, what's the matter?"

A hard shake of his head, he pushed away the cloth. "I'm all right. Sorry." He focused on the image of the white starched table linen and breathed. Color returned to his cheeks. "This is embarrassing, Emily. It's happened before but never in public."

"Can you tell me, my love?"

Silent at first, a chip in the armor he covered himself with fell away, then another, and there in the heart of Jerusalem with his bride he began to speak.

"I was the oldest of five children. I was supposed to protect the kids and our Mom from him." He lifted his gaze to meet hers. "Our father was an alcoholic, a bully. Sober during the week, the man had to work, but come Friday, he'd roar his way home and God help anyone who got in the way. The neighbors were good. They'd take turns hiding the little ones after I'd bring them over but Mom," he squeezed her hand, "she'd stay at home and he'd take it out on her. He beat her, Emily, our Mother, and there wasn't anything I could do about it until I was strong enough to stand up to him." He shivered although it was warm in the restaurant and they were drinking hot coffee.

"What did you do, Pat?" She was almost afraid to ask.

She could see the memories take hold as he described the final confrontation in the kitchen of the tenement apartment facing the drunken father. "I held a metal pipe in both hands, told him I'd kill him if he ever hurt her or any of us again. And he laughed at me. So I swung it and smashed it across his head." He turned away from the sight and looked at Emily.

"That's it? That's the whole story? What became of him?"

Patrick lifted her hand to his mouth and kissed each finger. "He was never the same after that. No one knew. We continued to live in that shabby little place with no good memories until he died. One big happy family."

"What did he die from?"

Tasting a chocolate pastry the waiter set before him, Pat said, "Cerebral hemorrhage." He offered a forkful of pastry to

Emily. Automatically she opened her mouth but later couldn't recall what it tasted like.

"How old were you?"

"Eleven."

"Oh, Pat."

"I was very tall for my age."

She sat very still, no longer aware of the exotic restaurant, strains of classic guitar rising from the street below. A cool autumn breeze caused to wrap the flowered shawl around her shoulders. Alert, the waiter moved to shut the French doors but Pat waved him away. He reached for Emily's hands.

"I've upset you, my darling." She patted his hands in response and shook her head.

"This is part of you, part of what you are. It explains why you are so protective."

She held his hand while he settled down, his serious side revealed. Now she understood why he wanted her to learn martial arts. He wanted to protect her and that was wonderful. They'd have the rest of their lives to discuss what was in their hearts and minds.

She leaned close kissing him, licking his lips, parting them in search of the chocolate. "Hmm. You finished the pastry, you ate the whole thing, didn't you? Greedy, didn't save any for the little wife."

"Emily," His voice was hoarse, "what the hell are you doing? I have a serious erection and the waiter hasn't brought the bill yet."

"Oh dear, so he hasn't." She slipped off her sandal and placed a silken hose clad foot over his crotch. "Yes, indeed, you have a serious you-know-what. How in the world did that happen, you horny man. Ask the waiter to bring another chocolate pastry and then the check."

This evening had taken on a different direction, one Emily hadn't foreseen. She felt like a detective, uncovering layers of her new husband.

While she enjoyed the pastry, Pat returned to his interest in Israel.

"Okay if we return to the sex thing after we leave here? My mind is on a roll. It's not often I want to unleash."

She nodded, happy to listen and savor the chocolate at the same time.

"Do you know there are more people walking around here with numbers tattooed on their wrists than any other place in the world?"

"No. I'm embarrassed to say I never thought about."

"It's true. I see crowds of men and women in shops, at work, trying to live normal lives, and I know that many of them suffered at the hands of others who believed themselves to be superior. It makes my blood boil, Emily, that unspeakable atrocities were condoned with a terrifying contempt for human life.

"Oh, Pat. We've been so wrapped up in each other and we never spoke of the outside world."

He went on. "Who changed The Golden Rule to read 'Do unto others before they do it to you'? A peaceful, caring world isn't possible."

"Pat, you mentioned suitable punishment before. I believe in an eye for an eye and no more. That's in the Old Testament, did you know that?"

"No, I didn't, but I believe in that too."

Samuel came to their table. "Everything was to your liking?"

The heavy atmosphere cleared out and smiles returned to the Corwin's. Promise of good things to follow uppermost in their minds.

"Dinner was superb, the service impeccable. You spoiled us with Dom Pérignon. Thank you, dear friend, for everything," Pat said.

Emily extended her hand and the courtly Samuel bent to kiss it. As he straightened, he made the smallest of gestures to Pat, who rose and followed Samuel out of the room without a backward glance at his wife. She was mystified as to what had taken place without a word, some form of communication between old friends. It was a bit rude to exclude her with no explanation. She didn't want to spoil the evening. On the other hand, she didn't want Pat to think he could just leave her like that. She stewed, played with her mirror, applied fresh lipstick, and finally walked out to the balcony where she was caught up in the night sounds and lights of Jerusalem.

Lost in reverie, thoughts far away of Larry and Mark

Wagner. They would have been more considerate. She couldn't picture Mark ever forgetting about her, even for a few minutes. A touch on her shoulders, kisses on cheeks brought her back to the present. Pat returned. Honeymoon resumed. She felt him press his hardness against her backside, fingertips caressing her waist, her bottom, and she turned and embraced him, a full body hug. Aware of a thickness inside his jacket, she was about to ask what it was when Samuel's deep voice called out.

"My driver will return you to The Arcadia now. I hope to see you again before your holiday ends."

She let go of the past and lived for the moment.

Chapter 18

After another delicious night of love making, Patrick rose early in high spirits after the brief meeting with Samuel. Now he would fulfill his mission and be free the rest of the week. He showered, dressed in a charcoal gray suit, starched white shirt, and power red tie. Attaché case in hand, he headed for the door, commitments on his mind. A compulsion to observe his wife stopped him in mid-stride. She slept, stretched out under the white blanket, long hair loose over the pillow and he was leaving her without a kiss, a touch, a something. He dropped the case, hurried over to the bed, and caressed his bride. Even in sleep, Emily smiled in response to his warmth.

"I'll be back in a couple of hours," he whispered. "Later, we can walk to the Walled City of Old Jerusalem. Once you've been there, it will be with you all your life. Guaranteed."

"The only guarantee I'll ever need is that you'll be with me the rest of my life," she murmured, rolling over.

An hour later, Emily was ready to explore. It would be an adventure to go out by herself. She dressed conservatively, as Pat had advised, in a long denim skirt and matching long sleeved shirt. Sneakers on, she headed out the door.

Ten minutes passed and from the front desk, Norith watched an anxious Emily return. "Shalom. May I be of assistance? I promised Patrick I would be your guide while he conducts business."

Emily was relieved. "Shalom and thanks for your kind offer. I didn't realize that most of the street signs are written with Hebrew symbols and the map confused me. I was lost minutes after I left here."

Norith laughed, her white and gold smile displayed.

"This happens all the time. Ben Ari will be in charge while you and I go to Jaffa Street. This is a most interesting place to shop and see ordinary people going about their daily chores. You are dressed appropriately for this excursion. Since you have not had breakfast, we may buy food from the vendors. This will be an experience for you as well."

Emily listened to Norith with interest. Somebody pinch me and I mean right now, she thought. In Jerusalem with a Sabra, a native born, who undoubtedly served two years in the Israeli Army, and going out on the town like friends. Terrific.

"Thanks. You saved the day for me. Ben Ari will take over while you're out and he won't mind?"

"Ben Ari is my husband. We work together and share tasks just as we did in the Army."

The women walked out the door, and waved Shalom to the handsome young man. They moved through the crowded streets at as brisk a pace as they could manage. Norith knew everyone. She nodded her head in greeting, and pointed out places of interest.

The sunshine felt wonderful after the endless travel of the day before. Was it only yesterday, they boarded the El Al plane and behaved so scandalously? She wondered if hidden cameras caught them and would they be allowed on the return flight. Her mind wandered for a moment. She missed Pat even though he'd come back soon.

Norith tugged at her. "Wake up, Emily. This is the famous Jaffa Street Market. Stay close to me. Hang your bag over your neck and under one arm, like this." She demonstrated with her own shoulder bag.

"This is like parts of Jacksonville, only more exotic."

Norith laughed. "If I were in Florida, I would think it to be exotic."

Open stalls jammed with merchandise lined the street. Throngs of shoppers chatted in loud voices, fast-everything was fast-language spoken so quickly. Emily wondered how they understood each other, or if they did. Maybe that's why there was always war. No one understood what the other guy said.

"First let us get you something to eat. Will you taste native food?"

"I'm game as long as you tell me what it is."

"Game? What does that mean?"

"It means I'm willing try anything and I trust you, so lead the way." She pulled Norith's arm."I really am not too adventurous about food but I will try."

"Follow me and you will taste baba-ganouj."

"Sounds like a curse word. What is it?"

"Mashed eggplant and tahini. Delicious. With a slice of Turkish bread and hot tea served from a samovar, you will be satisfied."

"Okay, if you say so."

The women giggled like young girls as they made their way to the best baba-ganouj in Jerusalem. True to the advertising, it was the best. Emily actually had a few bites and lived to tell Pat about it later.

After quick street dining, she wanted to see native-made clothing, something special to bring home. They looked through round racks of cotton outfits and Norith spied the most perfect blouse and skirt in shades of brown that matched Emily's eyes. She pulled it off the rack, held it up to Emily's slim shape and Emily nodded yes.

Norith took over. In rapid Hebrew, she gestured with hands, shoulders, and head; she gave the shopkeeper a fierce look, threw the outfit back on the rack, grabbed Emily's hand and stormed away from the stall. The shopkeeper ran after her. He cajoled, pleaded, and escorted the women back to the stall. Norith winked at Emily to show it was a game they played. She knew how to play very well.

The transaction cost fifteen shekels although the price tag said thirty.

Counting her money, Emily handed it to the man. As the shopkeeper reached out, his shirt sleeve pulled back and inked numbers were revealed on his exposed forearm. She looked at the man, and saw him as a person for the first time.

He was maybe in his late sixties, stooped in the shoulders with a plump, old man's belly. Scraggly gray hair, a skull cap perched on his head, and pale blue eyes hidden behind steel rimmed bifocals completed the external picture. What lay inside was his business but Emily knew from books, television, and movies, that this man was a Holocaust survivor. He conducted his life on this sunny day, business as usual.

Hugging the purchase close to her body as they made their way out of the Market, Emily knew she'd think of Norith every time she wore it. It was a symbol of friendship. The fact that

Norith had taken the morning off to show her around meant the world to her.

"Norith, might you and Ben Ari ever come to Florida?"

"This is not possible. We were in New York several years ago and enjoyed plays on Broadway. We shopped, went to a hotel management convention. We especially liked the ballet. Dance is an international language. But Florida? No."

"If you ever do, you'll stay with us. We'll show you a tropical paradise you haven't seen before. Okay?"

Norith was very pleased. "Okay," she said. "Now we must hurry. Patrick plans to take you to the Old City."

At the hotel, Norith transformed into innkeeper mode and Emily hurried to the suite where she hoped her husband was waiting. She recalled pearls of wisdom from her dear Mom. "Always keep your man waiting just a little while," she said so many years ago. "That way he'll always be eager to see you. But don't keep him waiting too long. Remember, there are a lot of pretty girls out there." Funny how her words came back at unexpected moments. Hey Mom, look at me. I'm on my second honeymoon. You'd like him, Mom.

The room key turned and she tiptoed in. Pat was at the desk, absorbed in work. Emily approached from behind and placed her hands over his eyes.

"Guess who?" she said. "Sorry I don't have any roses but you get the idea?"

He covered her hands with his and swiveled the chair to face his bride. Pulling her onto his lap, he rained feathery kisses all over her face. Ravenous for her, his passion high, he licked her skin, the inside of her mouth until she writhed in response. Then she molded her body to him and moaned. Over and over, he ran his fingers through her light hair. Somehow their clothes came off, although she noticed this time Pat was careful to empty the contents of his jacket into the attaché case and lock it before they were on the Persian rug.

"Shall we, to the bed?" she said.

"Shall we, what to the bed?" he said.

A routine from a Woody Allen movie they loved. They made a wild dash for the bedroom. At some point during the lovemaking, she wondered if she'd closed the door when she entered the suite. In the urgency of the moment, all was forgotten.

After yet another shower, they dressed for the afternoon's excursion to the Old City. Entering the living room, they found the door open, a tray of falafel, sour cream, chopped lettuce and olives, and a bottle of red wine on the table.

"Look's like a Good Samaritan was here while we were otherwise engaged."

"Yes, it does. Obviously someone heard about the hungry couple down the hall and came to the rescue."

"May as well enjoy the generosity of the house. Let's eat."

"Falafel," declared Emily, "is my new most favorite food." As she poured the wine she asked about Pat locking up his papers. "Were you concerned that someone might search our room?"

He gave her a blank look and she could see he didn't like her asking questions so she changed the subject. There were changes to be made but slowly. Don't rush.

They agreed the honeymoon was progressing nicely. It was only Day Two.

They thanked their benefactors profusely, and walked toward the Walled City. Emily brought a shawl to cover her head when they went into a sacred section. A fragrance filled the air and she tried to guess the source. Her nostrils worked overtime, as she sniffed all around like a puppy.

"I love your lack of inhibitions, always ready for adventure, always eager for fun," Pat said.

She stopped, pointed to low rosemary bushes growing wild along the sidewalks everywhere. Reached down to pluck a leaf but before she could, He pulled her away.

"Everything that grows in this land is precious. Better not to touch. Just let your senses be filled with the joy of being here."

Emily reached up and kissed his cheek. They held hands and entered the Old City through the Jaffa gate.

"The air is different in here. Maybe it's my imagination, but it feels as though we just traveled five thousand years back in time."

She caught their reflection in a large brass plaque on the wall of a shop. "We look the same."

"What do you mean?"

"We took two steps through the gate and I don't know why, but I feel like it's not modern times anymore."

Pat smiled. "You're caught up in the aura, that's all. This is another reason why we're here. I wanted to share Israel with you. I knew you'd wrap this country around you the way I did on my first visit."

"Right again, my husband. If you keep second guessing me like this, I'll have to wrap myself around you once more before the day ends."

He stopped, became serious. "We're here. Through the dark corridor ahead is the Western Wall."

"Pat, I've been meaning to ask you about your personal interest in this country. Are you Jewish?"

He led Emily to a quiet corner. "Last night I revealed something about growing up in the Midwest and this is an odd place to have a discussion, so I'll be brief."

She looked at him, a huge question mark in her eyes. "I thought you'd say no I'm not and we'd keep walking."

"No, I'm not," Pat said. "All my life I never felt a sense of being accepted, of being loved for who I am. There was a warmth I lacked. I never trusted anyone and always held a big part of me in reserve."

"Honey, I never felt that about you. We couldn't be together if you weren't the way you —"

He interrupted. "That's how I was before we met. The years in Israel opened up my life. New acquaintances became friends. The sociologist in me renewed interest in learning this culture and the history of the country. Best of all, I felt myself change. Slowly, I allowed these people into my narrow little life. I'm even closer to my daughter now, and that's a plus. Amanda knows she has a father she can talk to and turn to, if need be. Now, can you understand why this faraway place is special for me?"

"In a way, yes. We'll talk about this a lot more, dear heart." She hugged him. "Now, before we see the Western Wall, tell me why it's so important, okay?"

"Okay. It'll be an overview, as a professor says the first day of class. The Wall is Judaism's holiest site. I read that in a guide book." They smiled at his comment.

"This Wall is what's left of King Herod's temple," he continued. "I could give a lecture on the importance of it, but we'll save that for a cold night by the fire, if you're still interested. It's been an established prayer site since the 13th century and is the largest outdoor synagogue in the world."

"Thank you, professor. Now, shall we, to the wall?"

An armed guard leaned against a wall. His posture was casual but the ammunition belt across his chest, grenade at his waist, and a machine gun in hand, indicated that he was anything but casual.

They passed the guard and walked into brilliant sunshine. The world sparkled as if freshly washed. The ancient wall was on the left. A divided section with folding chairs faced the wall.

Pat whispered, "Men sit to the left, women to the right."

People sat and stood; they waited as if a performance were about to begin. Many languages were spoken in hushed tones. Emily felt timid when Pat moved to the men's side. She observed the women acting out the old world ritual; shawls covered bowed heads, prayer books in hands some unlined, some gnarled. Tears trickled down many cheeks, some faces were radiant. She saw people write on small scraps of paper and remembered what Pat told her. Notes to departed loved ones are tucked into spaces between the Wall's bricks, like a post office with a direct route to heaven.

As Emily walked to a seat, she passed a young woman in a passionate embrace with an armed soldier. Her body pressed tightly to him and displaced his rifle to the side of his body. He must be on a break, Emily thought.

She rummaged through her back pack for a pen and paper. Her mind wandered to another part of her life as she wrote: My dearest Larry, I feel your presence here. You're with me and happy I'm not alone anymore. Thank you for sending Patrick. You knew I was ready to let you go. Folding the note into the smallest possible form, Emily walked to the Wall. Bits of paper stuck out from between the bricks. One tiny crevice caught her attention and she knew that was where the note should go.

She touched the Wall and heat spread up her arm, her whole body warmed and a feeling of peace enveloped her. Emily leaned her forehead against the Wall, then turned and searched for Pat. He rose from his seat and met her at the back. Without a word, the

Starting Over

Corwin's left the sacred place, arms around each other.

    A FAX marked URGENT waited for Pat when they entered the hotel.

    "Oh no, what does it say?"

    Frowning, he read aloud.

    "Sorry to interrupt honeymoon. Client of some importance demands your attention. This is a big one. A bonus for your inconvenience."

    "It's signed by William Hays, senior member of the law firm I work for." He shredded the FAX letting the strips fall to the floor until it looked like confetti. "Emily, I'm so sorry." It was obvious he hated when things got out of his control. "It's probably another of those guilty investment brokers I'll have to defend. Oh no. I shouldn't have said that."

    "Listen to me," her voice strong, "I'm disappointed too but it's not your fault. You call the airline while I pack." She started down the hall to their room then turned back. "What do they say here? Oh yes. Next year in Jerusalem."

Chapter 19

"That was a really short honeymoon," Pat said as they waited in the customs line at the Jacksonville Airport. "I'll make it up to you, Sweetheart. Let's plan a vacation for spring. We'll go wherever you want."

"Pat honey, don't feel guilty about cutting our trip short. On the plus side, it's great to know you're so valuable to the firm. I already have a plan on how to spend the bonus promised by Mr. Hays."

Emily was exhausted after the whirlwind trip. Pat, fresh with eyes that sparkled, kissed her forehead.

"I have an idea. Let's use the bonus toward the house."

"I was thinking more of something to wear."

He looked at her as if she'd said something foolish.

"I'm kidding. Spend it on the house. Right now, I'm too tired to think clearly." She looked at all the weary travelers. "The line is fast. We've nothing to declare so unless they frisk me and search my bags, we should be home in two hours. You called the limousine?"

"Yes, someone will be here." He leaned close to whisper in her ear. "I may have to frisk you when we get home to make sure you didn't smuggle anything into the country."

She perked up long enough to reply. "I will happily submit to your sense of precaution after a hot bubble bath and a glass of wine, Sir."

Chapter 20

"Meg, pick up. It's Mom."

"Mom, are you all right? What's wrong? Are you still married? Why are you calling from Jerusalem?"

"Honey, calm down. Everything's wonderful and I'm calling from home. We got in late last night. There was an emergency at the firm and Patrick is needed for a new client. The good news is that he'll get a bonus."

"Excellent Mom. Actually I was worried about you being there. Are there armed soldiers all over the place?"

Emily smiled. Ever since her Dad died, Meg had been fiercely protective of her, like a mother bear watching over her cub. "Yes, but I feel safe with Pat. Your Mom's in good hands, not to worry."

An audible sigh of relief. "I'm happy you're back, Mom. I missed you."

"There is some exciting news, honey."

"Oh Mom, don't tell me you're —"

Emily laughed. "Don't be a goof. I'm a bit old for that. Pat and I decided to renovate my house and we'll ask Jake to do the job. Every corner of the house holds memories of your Dad and you kids. Before I met Pat, those memories were a comfort to me. We want to change things around to make the house ours. Not just mine. And the property is valuable since its beachfront."

"Great idea. I'll tell Jake to call for a meeting with you. I want the house to be ours someday a long, long time from now. Gotta run. Can't be late for school. Love you."

"Love you, too."

Email showed Congrats on Wedding from Erle. What a pal. Widows Group sent a musical card. She stretched, put on a Jerry Lee Lewis DVD, and felt a grin coming on. Life was good.

After running the next morning, Emily drove to the Dojo and had an intense training session in Tai Kwan Do. She was already a yellow belt working to advance to orange level. Board breaking proved to be easy enough, boards not thick, concentration needed and she had plenty of that. She worked on kicks, stances and basic self defense moves.

Sparring was a different matter. Facing off hand to hand with an opponent was a difficult skill, one she had to overcome in order to move up. No fun lying flat on your back staring up at a kid much smaller who just knocked your feet from under you. She had to yell louder, move faster. Soon, she promised herself.

School had begun, the talent looked promising for the new season and the house project would begin within a week. Everything good. Except for Pat's new client. He opened up about defense of clients he knew were guilty. Mixed feelings especially after the last one. They were comfortable and happy together.

He was secretive sometimes and once Emily woke in the middle of the night and heard him speaking what sounded like Hebrew. The next morning, she asked if his Israeli friend called and he said no. As far as Emily knew, that was the first lie. And she didn't know why. A month went by, another quick trip to the Middle East and Patrick came home quite upset. Again, he didn't confide in her.

The next morning, Emily decided to mend fences. She tiptoed from slid out of bed, not to disturb Pat and brewed his favorite coffee. The aroma woke him before her warm body spooned close, did.

"Well, good morning, sunshine."

"And to you, my husband."

He sipped the steaming brew and kissed her. Emily loved the second hand taste coming from his mouth.

"I've missed you," she said.

"Not anymore," he said, and her nightie was off and over her head, their warm bodies exploring each other as if new territory had just been discovered. Maybe it was, she thought, later. New territory on how to overcome distance, secrets, whatever. Marriage required a lot of energy to keep life happy.

Meanwhile, under the covers, Pat found Emily's silken folds and did some delicious exploring on his own. Coffee lost heat. But not the loving couple. Time slowed. Emily sucked Pat's neck leaving little love bites and cried out for more when he thrust into her all the way in, then out and back in.

"Don't stop."

He panted. "I have to get to the office." Thrusting again and again.

"Call. Say you're running late."

"What about you?"

"I called a substitute while you were sleeping."

They laughed and made love most of the morning until most of the fences mended.

Satisfied finally, he left for work.

An unexpected call from Lola, Emily's artist friend, changed any plans she might have made for the day.

"Come right over. I'd love to see you."

Soon a crunch of crushed shells on the driveway announced Lola's arrival. Tall, pretty although a bit heavier since the wedding, she climbed out of the red BMW and posed.

"Tada," she said.

They hugged. "I brought a wedding gift for you." She opened the trunk and hauled out a large paper wrapped rectangle.

"Let me guess," Emily said. "Must be the earrings I admired a long time ago." More laughter and they carried in the package.

"Let me explain how this came to be. But first some iced sweet tea, please." Lola dropped her large raffia handbag on a rattan table and followed Emily to the kitchen.

"Just so happens, like all good Floridians, there's a pitcher right here." Emily opened the fridge, removed a pitcher and poured two glasses full of the pick-up drink.

"Lots of traffic coming down from town," Lola said, swigging a huge swallow.

"Stay over tonight and we'll catch up."

"It's a thought. Thanks."

They moved back to the entrance and Lola undid the wrapping as she spoke. "I was in my studio working when suddenly I dropped the brush and picked up a pencil and began to sketch. Then the pencil dropped from my hands with a crash. How could a pencil weighing less than an ounce make so much noise? I had to towel off and when I wiped my face and hands, I looked at the sketch. It was unlike anything I'd ever drawn. Emily, you've seen my work."

She nodded, intrigued by the story, wondering what it had to do with her.

"Everything I draw has a photographic look. In all my forty some years

I've painted realistically. Yet I had drawn an impressionistic rendering of several Emily's, starting small and growing with a fierce energy. Not in pencil but in oil."

The canvas was about five feet tall and four feet wide. An odd shape. Emily recognized herself painted in shades of purple, thick slabs of oil in a frenzy. Nothing peaceful to look at but rather a palpable vibrancy emitted from the canvas. Three shadowy male images appeared behind and through her. It was exciting and disturbing at the same time.

"Emily, when I looked at it, my first thought was that it was startling and goddamned good. I had to shake my head to clear it. I needed a drink, maybe two. My hands ached to begin what would become a wedding gift for you. I would call it "Emerging Woman." Where the title came from is a mystery to me, as much a mystery as the strange interlude."

Lola stopped to finish her tea and catch her breath.

"Before I say another word, I want to thank you for the lovely tea but at this moment I crave a glass of wine. Is Chardonnay in the fridge?

"Yes, of course."

Emily rose from the couch feeling shaky as she walked to the kitchen. The painting had a profound effect on her and she was eager to hear the rest of the story. Never a dull moment when Lola was around. She poured two glasses of wine and returned to the living room. Lola's head was snuggled into a paisley brown throw pillow, eyes closed. She blinked as Emily approached and she reached for the wine.

"Emily, it's so good to see you again. I will stay overnight if the offer still holds. When does Pat return?"

Her face flushed with memories of why Pat would be late.

"He didn't leave until noon so he won't get home for quite a while. We'll have plenty of time to catch up and have a simple meal later. Does pasta sound good?"

"Sounds good to me. You sly rascal. Was he delayed this morning by a pressing engagement?"

They laughed at the innuendo like two goofy teenagers, Emily blushed from embarrassment. She hadn't shared intimate details with anyone since she met Pat.

"Ain't love grand," Lola said. "All that sex available. I envy you."

"What happened to the great looking guy you brought to the wedding?"

"Another failed romance, sorry to say. Maybe my work gets in the way. Maybe my deodorant let me down. Who knows? The good news is the commissions come rolling in. Word of mouth, the human network, whatever. I'm painting my ass off and I love it. Actually all this work keeps me sitting and my butt reflects the lack of exercise. You, my skinny friend, look terrific."

"Thanks for the compliment. A little exercise wouldn't hurt you but you're as beautiful as ever. How about this for a plan?"

"I'm glad to see you haven't forgotten how to take charge."

"Fat chance of that. Sorry about the F word. Let me show you around the house and we'll find a place to hang the wonder picture. Then a little work-out, I can demonstrate some martial arts technique, have dinner, and talk some more. How does that sound?"

"Martial arts? Since when?"

"Many months of Tai Kwan Do. I'm an orange belt now."

"Good for you. I'm yours but don't overdo it. Maybe I'll just watch."

The women walked from room to room and Lola dropped her gear bag in the guest room. Emily gave her shorts and a sweatshirt and everything she'd need for the night. Lola changed and they met in the kitchen where she set the table while Emily gathered the fixings of a pasta meal.

"If anything Emily, you're even more organized now as a married lady. Pat must love that."

"I've always had to be since I'm a teacher. It's essential to keep order for Pat and easy for me so I do it. No big deal. My New Year's resolution is to insist that I have more time for personal growth and pursuits. Before we met, I signed up for computer class and finished it in spite of his time demands on me."

95

"I hear you. Avoiding cop-outs heads my list of resolutions. Are you happy? Happy with Patrick and this second time around?"

She didn't answer right away. "Mostly yes. You can't have everything, I guess. It's not like when I was young and getting married the first time. Compromises have to be made. He carries a lot of baggage from his past. But mostly life is very good with him."

Picking up the painting, Emily led the way to the new exercise room.

Lola's eyes widened as she took in this room. Not at all like the other warm, cozy rooms in the house. This room spelled purpose, goals, achievements.

"I do see a great spot for the picture."

Lola pointed to a place on the wall, lifted the picture, and they agreed. Emily found a hammer, a hook and nail and the picture was hung. Emerging Woman had a home.

After a late pasta supper washed down with too much Merlot, the women curled up on the couch like two cats before the dying embers of the fire. Lola inhaled deeply through her nose, holding her breath before she exhaled. Emily recognized the relaxation technique and wondered what was on her friend's mind. She knew she'd find out soon.

"I never told you this but I'm just drunk enough to confess. Her voice husky, drenched with food and drink.

Here it comes, thought Emily. She smiled, nodded to encourage her. The hour was late, they were tired, but they might not see each other for a while. Better seize the moment while it was there.

Tears filled Lola's big hazel eyes and spilled down full cheeks. She was in total disarray, unlike the perfect polished friend of months ago, long blonde hair hung limp like a damp mop, nose reddened by crying and all the wine.

An attempt to comfort Lola for God knew what, was rejected.

"I actually met Patrick at a party two years ago in Jax and I wanted him, went after him and you got him and I feel guilty about hating you for that. He doesn't even remember me."

"You hate me? Even now?"

"No. Of course not." She hiccupped. The wine repeated. "I'll never drink again. It's just that the sex was so good and I miss it."

"You had sex with my husband?"

"That's what big people do, you know. And he wasn't your husband then. You didn't even know him."

"How many times did you go out with him? I thought it was a casual relationship."

"It was on his part. Three times." She blotted the tears with her sleeve.

They were quiet for a long minute. Emily started giggling. Lola joined her and they laughed and couldn't stop.

"It's okay that you slept with my husband who wasn't my husband then. And it's okay that you hated me but don't hate me now. Just don't have sex with Pat anymore, okay?"

That said, they stumbled down the hall still laughing and bid each other a silly good night.

Midnight. In the shower, Emily thought about the long day as she scrubbed her back with a long handled brush. Begun with sex in the bedroom, bathroom and once on the floor, Lola showing up with the amazing painting, and an evening of reminiscing. Wonderful.

The brush soothed her tired muscles. She added soap and moved the brush around to her front, starting with shoulders and arms, headed south to breasts. She guided the brush lower and sighed with pleasure. When did she ever get to be such a horny woman? Pat should be home any minute. If he's not too tired…A light knock on the shower door startled her.

His voice called, "Guess who?"

Emily's heart pounded with excitement. Through the translucent glass, she saw he was naked. He stepped into the shower and embraced his wife. Emily discarded the brush as she threw her arms around his neck, and wrapped her legs around his hips. He entered her and moaning together, they came.

The next morning it was business as usual. Her friend had left and the loving sweet husband turned his eye to a distant place she had no part of. That night, things between them changed for a short while.

"Let's take a walk on the beach," Pat said, after dinner. Emily agreed and they walked out the back, stepped on wide wooden planks down through the dunes and on to the beach.

Pat was silent for a while as he set a brisk pace. Then a torrent of words released like a breaking dam. He'd held himself so tight all his life, played his cards close to the vest, feelings hidden to protect himself from hurt, first from his father, then from his wife. Now at last he was free to let go without recrimination.

"We've had so many good days, months and our future is bright. I want you to know that I'm through looking in the rearview mirror at my past. It's dangerous doing that. You miss what's right out in front of you, within reach. I'm through beating myself up over well-meant intentions gone wrong. I really tried to be the good son, the good husband, the good father. Now I promise you, my precious wife..." Pat stopped walking and faced her. Tears trickled down her cheeks. He brushed them away with his fingertips. "I'll love you and take care of you always. You've freed me from the prison I created by loving me unconditionally. You accepted me from the beginning at face value for who I am and who I could become. Thank you, Emily. I'll never let you down." He gave her the boyish smile she loved.

She flung her arms about his neck and hung on for dear life. Then she released him and hand in hand, they continued walking.

Life with Patrick see-sawed and one night loud voices woke her. She felt the bed for Pat. Not there. Heart pounding she sat up, bedside clock glowed a green two a.m. Chilled, she tip-toed to the hall and listened. Two men arguing, one sounded like Samuel-heavy accent. Hollow-electronic speaker-phone sound. Pat in his office on speaker-phone with Samuel. Her sleepy brain woke up fast. Pat saying something like, You said last time was the last. I won't do it again. Samuel urgently said, You must, one more time, I promise on the souls of my family. We need you. I need. Pat groaned, I trusted them. You are the only one I do it for. When? Samuel, Tomorrow.

Emily ran into the office catching Pat unaware of her presence. "What's wrong, sweetheart?"

He clicked off the speaker. "Nothing. Go back to bed."

"I heard you talking to Samuel. It was him wasn't it?"

"No. I have to leave early tomorrow. Come." He hung up. He tucked her in, ignored questions as he packed a carry-on bag taking with him a small packet she had seen before. All this accomplished in the dark room as if he had done it all his life. For all Emily knew, he had. Who was he? She slept. In the morning he was gone, a terse note said he'd come back in two days.

When he returned, silent about where he'd been and why, he watched television news constantly, something he seldom did. He didn't go in to corporate headquarters, choosing to work from his office at home. He ate little, communicated less. Stymied, Emily didn't know what to do except continue to work and ride it out.

On the fourth day, she was at the computer, when she heard him cry out during a news broadcast. She hit Save and ran to his office where Pat lay curled on the carpet. The impeccable anchorman with perfect diction described a bombing in a refugee camp in the Middle East. "At the scene live," he said, and another reporter showed a school leveled, all inhabitants killed. Small bodies scattered on the ground, blown apart, pieces found miles away. A bereft mother cradled what was left of her child, her grief universal.

Emily held him, not understanding the powerful reaction to the tragedy. "Did you know people in the settlement?" Nothing. "Please talk to me." He lay limp in her arms. The warm room, her body heat, couldn't stop his trembling. "I must call a doctor," and she rose to leave. The first sign of life from him. A steely grip held her in place.

"No doctor. This will pass." His private phone rang, answer machine picked up, Samuel's voice. Pat screamed, "No. Liar. You lied to me." Tears streamed. He said, "My friend, mentor, he called me little brother and lied, Emily. At least my father never lied."

Samuel left messages every day but Pat refused to speak to him. He never spoke to him again.

Chapter 21

Silently, Emily and Patrick dressed for a run. Saturday morning, stiff breeze on the water, tide out for now. Dark and chilly. No fishermen, no other runners. Just the Corwin's, secrets again interfering with their love and friendship.

They started at an easy pace and Emily picked it up moving with her usual long legged stride, graceful and smooth. Pat moved up next to her and kept the beat. Slap, slap against damp sand, into the wind. She upped the ante and pulled way ahead; not a race just a need to go faster. She didn't realize he'd fallen way behind until she glanced back. Pat was jogging, moseying along, not like himself and she kept going, going until he was a speck in the distance and still she ran.

High on his perch, Clifford saw an opportunity. The honeymooners on the beach. Juiced on black coffee, obsessed with his Goddess and his plan, he grabbed keys to the restored dune buggy he treasured and headed out for a little ride. Gunning the motor, the buggy sailed over the dunes onto the flat hard packed sand. Course set straight ahead for, oh my, if it isn't his lawyer dear Patrick Corwin jogging alone and where oh where is she? Ah yes, far up the beach, the lonely quiet beach with no one around and only the fierce wind making all that racket.

Just a tap to send him sprawling, one tiny tap. Clifford Lansdale geared up high, pedal to the floor and headed straight for the target. Pat didn't even hear him coming. A slam in the middle of his back sent him flying backwards onto the hood. The lawyer slid almost face to face with the windshield, his eyes already unfocused. The buggy drove on coming to a stop at water's edge. Not quite what you had in mind, Cliffie. Breathing heavily, he climbed out of the buggy. Get him off, get him off. Using forgotten strength, driven by an adrenalin rush, he tugged at the bloodied body until it was thrown clear landing where waves pooled over it and the remains of the clever lawyer, Patrick Corwin, swayed gently with each ebb and flow of the sea.

The dune buggy continued up the beach, parking behind a large dune before the Goddess heard a sound. Old smartie Clifford got out and ran in the soft sand as fast as he could and just as he came near enough to touch her, she turned. Their eyes met for only a second. Beautiful. So close.

As his Goddess ran screaming for help all the way to the shape in the water, Clifford Lansdale hurried to the buggy and skirting the area, drove safely to his mansion.

Lights went on, one two, three and suddenly the whole beach lit up with the rising sun and sirens. Medics responding to neighbors calls. Woman screaming on the beach, body in the water. People poured out from expensive homes in the exclusive area, some curious, some wanting to help brought blankets.

Emily cried, waves mingled with tears as she touched Pat's face, blood soaked her hands, everything soaked with salt water and blood. His eyes were open. Her face bent close to his, she listened for breathing. Nothing. She felt for his heart. No beating. Cradling him in the shallow waves, she rocked back and forth, back and forth.

Sirens broke the silence but Emily didn't hear them. The ambulance stopped right next to her, flashing red light bathed Emily and Pat in a surreal glow. She didn't lift her head. Men and women rushed out, equipment in bags, a stretcher on wheels. She didn't move.

A voice said, "She's in shock. Somebody take her. Hurry."

A uniformed woman pried Emily's fingers from her husband and guided her away from him. Emily's hand gripped Pat's favorite cap not letting go.

"Do you hear me?" She didn't respond. "Get a blanket. Quick."

Wrapped in a blanket, Emily was led into the ambulance. She looked at her benefactor. "I saw a man," she said.

Outside, a medic examined Pat, checked for vital signs, found none. He shook his head.

Police arrived. Several patrol cars. Flashing lights. The whir, click sounds from a camera. The forensic Crime Specialist Investigator arrived and took charge. The Medical Examiner pronounced Pat dead. A detective took notes and asked for estimated time of death. The M.E. said, "Six fifteen. His watch stopped at 6:15.

Looks like he died right after he was hit. We'll know more after the autopsy."

Pat was zipped into a body bag and carried into the second ambulance.

"Who's on accident reconstruction today?"

"Klein. He'll love getting up early."

"We're lucky to have him. It wasn't so long ago we'd be tied up with measurements, calculations, and figuring distances in addition to all the paper work."

"Right. I'll save him a donut."

Detective O'Keefe introduce himself to Emily. "I'm sorry for your loss, Mrs. Corwin. I have to ask you a few questions. All right?" She nodded. "You told the medic you saw a man. Can you describe him?"

"I was way up there," she pointed to where a rock jetty formed, "running fast. I don't know why, but Pat," Emily sobbed, "slowed way down." O'Keefe offered her a tissue. She accepted it and wiped her eyes. "A man came close to me, older, big guy, wild looking. I only saw him for a minute. Uh. Glasses, wire frames, dark eyes, thin gray hair kind of long. My skin crawled and I looked back to call..." gulps of air, "I didn't see my husband but saw something, in the water, you know?"

"Do you know the man? Have you ever seen him before?" Emily shook her head no. "Who can I call to be with you, Mrs. Corwin? We may have to take you to the hospital just to make sure you're all right."

"No hospital. No."

"My daughter, Meg Thorne and Amanda Fitzgerald, Pat's daughter. Oh God, I'm the only parent left." Emily thought hard. Her mind was scrambled. "Professor Mark Wagner. He's my friend. He said to call any time, day or night if I needed him. He said he'd be open twenty four hours for me. The phone numbers are at home in my purse in a little book. We..."

She stopped again, realizing there was no 'we' anymore. Tears fell, a river full. She wondered if there was a well inside her and if it would ever run dry.

"Mrs. Corwin, I have to ask you one more thing." Emily looked up at him. "Does your daughter know Professor Wagner?"

"He's her Godfather. Oh, please call him first. If you can reach him, ask him to call Meg. It would be better than talking to a stranger."

"She needs a sedative," said the medic.

"No, no, no," Emily said. "Take me home. I live a mile or so down the beach, just past the rich folks neighborhood."

The detective said, "You may be suffering from shock and exposure, Mrs. Corwin. It's a good idea to let someone take care of you for a little while. My daughter was on the track team at the college about five years ago and she thought you were the greatest."

Mind in a muddle, Emily tried to focus. "O'Keefe. Nancy O'Keefe. Right? A terrific girl. How is she?"

He laughed. "The only hurdles she jumps right now are my grandkids. A boy and a girl."

She was on the way to the hospital, a blanket warming her, half dozing. Detective O'Keefe had conned her into going along with the medics if only for a little while. Then she was cold, so cold. She didn't know if she would ever be warm again. A blood pressure cuff was strapped to her arm. The medic took her pulse.

"You'll be taken to Community Hospital. I'll be there soon. Right now, I'll call your friend and if I can reach him, he'll tell your family to go to the hospital," Detective O'Keefe said. He talked with the medic. "Stay with her. And put her in a quiet room. When the family comes, she can go home if the doctor says she's well enough. I'll be there in an hour."

He left. The ambulance pulled away. Lights flashed, the siren wailed.

The word was out. Hot news. Someone, more than one, monitored 911 and police calls and phoned in the scoop to the powers that be. Reporters, mulled around cell phones in hands at the ready; videographers with camcorders shivered in the early morning chill; the local cable station sent a van complete with anchorwoman and hairdresser to cover the breaking news. Prominent Jacksonville lawyer died on St. Augustine Beach under suspicious circumstances. That's news. No one knew exactly what happened, but they were all there to find out and report. Circling the emergency entrance like birds of prey, they searched for a tasty morsel. First one gets the prize, the credit for a gift to John Q. Public. Give the people something to digest along with breakfast, to shake heads over, to be thankful it happened to someone else, and to wonder if these unfortunates were neighbors. The ambulance bearing Emily hadn't arrived, but the greeting committee was in place ready to do the job.

As the ambulance neared the emergency entrance, the medic asked Emily stay quiet on the stretcher. "Mrs. Corwin, reporters are out there and we want to protect you from all that commotion. I'm going to cover you completely and we'll go in fast. Okay?"

Emily agreed and lay back as the blanket descended. Then she began to scream. "I feel dead. Suffocating. No air under here. Can't breathe. Help." She thrashed, attempted to throw off the blanket. The medic loosened the cover and squeezed her hand.

"Sorry. Stay still for another minute and we'll get you into a quiet room. Your family will be here soon." He called, "Open the doors."

Cool air rushed in, shouts from everywhere, cameras whirred, voices with questions. She kept her eyes shut, stayed still, and she was airborne. Stretcher wheels moved fast, hit the pavement expertly steered and Emily was through the automatic doors, away from prying eyes. The blanket slipped off her face. Her eyes took in pale green walls, bright lights, the staff dressed in green scrubs and white uniforms busy with clipboards, phones to answer. A normal day for them. Antiseptic smells filled her nostrils in this world without Pat.

Her eyes closed, tears leaked out and trickled down her cheeks to soak into her already wet shirt. Pat, where are you?, her mind shouted. Too much to bear. Too much.

Wheeled into a private room, the door closed. Noise from the corridor shut out. Emily said, "Help me up, please. My girls have to see a healthy mother."

"Grab my arm," said the medic. "Here you go. Are you dizzy?"

"No." She sat in a visitors chair, Pat's cap clutched to her heart.

"Your blood pressure is fine now. Pulse is steady. Can I get you something before I leave?"

"What's your name? You've taken good care of me and I don't know your name."

"Elena," said the medic. "Would you like some coffee or tea?"

"Decaf tea, if that's possible, and thank you, Elena."

The medic headed for the door, turned back and said, "I'm sorry for your grief. You'll be in my prayers."

Emily was alone, the persistent chatter of the intercom for company.

"Calling Doctor Smith, Doctor Smith; calling Doctor Burke,

Doctor Burke..." The big clock on the wall hit seven. Forty six minutes ago, Pat was running. Now he was gone forever.

She must have dozed for a few minutes. A commotion in the hall, loud footsteps pounded and the door flung open. A disheveled Meg ran in, followed by husband Jake and Mark Wagner. Even at this early hour during an emergency, Mark was perfectly groomed. Meg fell to her knees, head in her mother's lap, her arms around her waist. A camera man pushed his way in, a voice called 'get the mother and child reunion' shot. Jake and Mark pushed them out. Jake made a grab for the camera but Mark pulled him away.

"It's his job. Nothing personal. Ugly, isn't it?"

Jake stood there, fists clenched, posture rigid with anger. He moved to Meg and his mother-in-law, and gathered them in his muscular arms.

"Mom, what happened?"

In a halting voice, Emily recounted the morning events. She wept. They cried with her. "I saw a man on the beach."

Mark said, "Who?"

"I never saw him before but I described him to Detective O'Keefe." Mark asked her to continue and she did between tears and sips of tea a nurse brought in. Meg wiped her mother's face with a wet wash cloth. She dabbed some moisturizer on her as well. When Emily told them about finding Patrick's body in the water, everyone took a deep breath. It was too painful. In an instant, all their lives changed.

Mark had more questions. "This man, have you ever seen him?" Emily shook her head no. "I'm sorry to ask but it's very important while details are fresh in your mind. All right?" She agreed. "What else can you remember about him, anything at all. You said there was eye contact for the briefest moment."

She was quiet, eyes squeezed tight. "His eyes were strange."

"In what way?"

"So huge, black. Stared without focus. I can't explain it," said Emily. "As if he knew me, wanted something from me."

"That's good. You're doing fine. I talked to the head nurse when I got here. As soon as you feel ready, the kids can take you home. I want to talk to the police on the scene. Maybe they found evidence, tire tracks, something. There's a lot of information to be gathered, but that's my job. I'll keep you in the loop. I'll go now and meet you at the house, make some calls, and consult with detectives I know. The

District Attorney is an old adversary. We've stayed on friendly terms."

Emily came out of the chair, face red with anger. "It must have been the man. They've got to find him, Mark. An eye for an eye. That's what I want. He can't go free. I know in my heart he killed Patrick."

No tears now. A cold look on her face. "I'll kill him myself if I find him."

Stunned by her outburst, Mark reached behind and closed the door. Noise from the corridor was shut off. He put his hand up in a quiet gesture.

"Don't say that in front of anyone. People will be watching you, ready to report anything you say." He beckoned the kids to move closer. Now they were in a tight circle. "Be discreet. Do not talk to reporters without talking to me first. Do not speak of revenge or imply those feelings. Your words will be twisted and misunderstood. Got that?"

"But we're the victims here. I don't understand," Emily said, fire in her eyes.

Mark held her by the shoulders. "Please trust me to find out what is going on."

"All right," Emily said. "Kids?" They agreed to follow his advice. "Mark, where is Pat, where did they take him? I want to see him."

"The coroner has work to do. They won't let you see him until later. I'd better leave and make the calls." He bent down and kissed her on the forehead. "Wait for Amanda and Mike. They'll be here any minute." He took Meg by the hand and led her outside the room. "Hang on to her, Meg. She needs all of us, but especially you."

Sobbing, Meg threw her arms around him. "I will, Uncle Mark, I will."

Emily chased after Mark and reached him just before he entered the elevator. She stood in front of her dear friend, Pat's blood dried on her running clothes. Resolute, wide awake in the present moment, a strength built inside her.

"All right, Emily. I'll help you in every way I can. Just like the old days." He hugged her tight.

"I'll wait for you at the house."

The elevator door opened. He got on, and turned to watch her as the door closed.

Emily strode back to the room dodging breakfast carts,

gurneys, wheel chairs. The hall was like rush hour with all the traffic. The door was open. Meg's arms were around Amanda, both girls in tears. Jake and Amanda's husband Michael looked through the window at the media vultures lusting after news. The brothers-in-law leaned toward each other, and murmured in low tones.

"Kids," Emily said, "my family." She opened her arms to them. The girls embraced her.

"Meg told you?" she asked Amanda.

"As best I could, Mom. They just got here."

"We'll leave in a minute and I'll tell you everything."

Amanda was speechless. Shocked with the hideous news, her face drained of color, knees buckled as she sank to the floor. Mike lifted her to the chair and Emily rang for a nurse. Meg ran into the hall, grabbed a small carton of apple juice from the breakfast cart, opened it, popped a straw in and gave it to Amanda.

"She didn't eat anything before we left," said Mike. "She's pregnant."

They were taken by surprise. Meg stared at Amanda, a secret grin on her face.

One door closes and another door opens. Oh God, Pat's first grandchild and he won't be here.

"I'm here," Emily said. "Your family is here."

The nurse bustled in, took blood pressure and pulse and pronounced both Amanda and Emily fit enough to leave.

"I have to call Tom and then we'll go," Emily said. Using the cell phone, she speed dialed her son. The phone rang once, twice, three times. She was impatient. Maybe he wasn't home. A sleepy voice answered. She pictured her son; puffy eyes, five o'clock shadow out-of-control, creased pillow case lines on his cheek. She hated to make this call.

Sounds of the phone falling, being picked up.

"Tom."

"Mom?"

"Yes." A pause.

"Something's happened to Pat."

"How did you know?"

"The last time you called this early was when Dad died."

"Yes. Can you come here soon, please?"

"I'll be there in two hours." An eloquent silence. "Is he dead, Mom?"

Emily gave a shuddering sigh. "Yes. One hour ago, we were on the beach, running. I didn't see it happen but I think a man hit him and drove away, killed him. I need you, Tom." Silence on the line. "Drive carefully."

"Ah, Mom. I love you."

"I know." She hung up. "Let's get out of here."

The family flanked Emily as the hospital doors swung open. Flashbulbs popped like tiny explosions in the crowd of reporters. A story of possible vehicular homicide on the beach had spread and they wanted to verify the rumor, hungered for names to put with the story. Microphones invaded their space as the family tried to walk through to the parking lot. Questions hurled through the air. Emily stopped. A microphone was thrust in her face and she wrenched it from the hand that held it.

"Stop shouting at us," she said to the crowd. Her electronic voice rang out in the morning air. "Have some respect for our grief. I know you're only doing your job but have some decency here."

The noise level dissipated, and then came to a halt. Grown men and women shuffled their feet like school kids reprimanded by a teacher.

Emily handed the microphone back to the reporter and the family made their way to the parking lot. Noise from the crowd welled up as they saw their prey escape.

Meg shook her head. "Life's not fair," she said to her husband. "Okay. Mom, go with Amanda and Mike. Lock the car doors before you're bothered again. We'll be at the house soon."

They drove north 'til they reached Atlantic View and soon they were home. Emily talked all the while, her arm around Pat's daughter. Half an hour later, Mike made a right turn onto the driveway to the old house.

Two policemen were at the front door in deep conversation with Mark Wagner. Serious faces on the men, as Mark was informed about evidence found at the scene, no doubt. Emily felt a measure of comfort with him in charge. He had always been a man of his word.

She got out of the car and Michael drove her car into the

garage.

"We'll need lots of parking room in the driveway for guests." Another wave of sadness hit her. She and Pat had talked about having a party. Not now. Not ever. No anniversary celebration. The Justice of the Peace pronounced them to be husband and wife, to love and to cherish, in sickness and in health, until death — the events of the morning played an endless loop in her mind.

As Emily approached the men, Amanda's hand in hers, she knew that to get through this day she couldn't look further than the next moment. The kids needed the last parent as a figurehead and all she wanted to do was curl into a ball and pray this time would pass. Instead she had to be Saint Emily. God forgive her but she was so tired of being strong.

"Emily, this is Officer Ben Moore. You met Officer O'Keefe. They are bringing me up to date with the latest information."

"Come in. The girls will make coffee."

She felt overwhelmed at being hospitable just then, but maybe it would help her get from one minute to the next. The men said coffee would hit the spot and Emily entered the house to continue her life.

"Mandy, please set out the coffee mugs, napkins, creamer and sugar bowl and anything else you can think of. There's a fresh fruit bowl in the fridge and some muffins we can heat. I'll put the coffee on."

Amanda didn't say a word. She was like a robot programmed to follow instructions. Emily led her to the family room where they'd be private. This sweet girl was an only child. At twenty seven, with both parents dead, she'd need a lot of tender loving care. Her husband, Jake, was a good guy. Pat is, was, Emily corrected herself, fond of his son-in-law.

"Mandy honey, this is the worst that could happen to us. We'll stick together and somehow we'll survive. We've all been through tragedy before. I want you to think of me as your second mom and your friend. Your baby will be my first grandchild. Mandy, look at me please." Emily turned Mandy to face her. The stony, frozen look was gone, replaced with melancholy.

"Mom, what's going to happen to me? I don't think I can live without my Dad. I love Jake but our baby won't know Dad and I don't know what to do."

Be strong, be strong. You can do it. Sounds at the door

distracted Emily. With unusual restraint, Meg and Jake entered the house, treading softly as if in a holy place. They were subdued unlike their boisterous happy selves. Emily watched them as if from a great distance. She had the old leaving-the-scene feeling and struggled to keep herself in the present. The aroma of fresh brewed coffee forced a sense of normal behavior.

"Meg, please ask Mark and the police to come in. Coffee's ready."

Her voice sounded too loud to her ears. This is home, she shouldn't feel like whispering, but she did. She'd been in this position before. When Larry died, everyone spoke in hushed tones as if they were in church or the library. It's natural, she guessed but she hated it. We're not going to wake anyone if we talk normally. Can't wake Pat. Oh no. Black humor and when was this merry-go-round mental conversation going to stop?

"Mandy, please help Meg with the breakfast things while I talk to the police. Then I must take a shower and straighten up the bedroom." She tried to gather scattered thoughts. "Honey, eat something and make sure the men have a bite, too. The expectant father has to keep his strength up." Emily attempted a laugh. It was feeble at best.

Emily went back to the family room. At the picture window, she pressed her face to the glass and looked out at the wide expanse of sand and flowers. Life was like that. Cyclical, round and round. It's here and then it's not. They had plans for this area. She couldn't carry them out alone. Didn't want to.

Thin hands pressed to her head. Held it tight in an effort to control runaway reflections. A deep breath followed by another, and she turned to face the day.

Sun streamed through the kitchen windows and bathed the room with a welcome warmth. No one sat at the big table. Maybe they believed that would be intrusive. She watched from the doorway. They stood in groups, talking in those same hushed tones while coffee and biscuits were consumed. When Emily came in, conversation ceased for a moment and then continued.

"Mom," said Meg. "Mandy fixed a plate for you. Just your style, too. Half a piece of toast with fruit jelly, a navel orange cut up in sections, and chamomile tea. Mom's a big eater," she said to the group.

"Thanks, girls." She took the offering, not knowing if she could eat. "Gentlemen, is there anything you want to ask me before you answer my questions?"

She gestured to the seats as she sat down. The men sat, one of them removed a note pad from his jacket.

"Thanks for your hospitality. We met your husband several times before working on cases."

Emily wondered where she was while Pat met with these policemen and realized she and Pat hadn't known each long enough to really get acquainted.

His partner nodded. "He was a good man. We're sorry for your loss. The beach is considered to be the safest place for pedestrians. Patrolled, safety zones. We're proud of our beaches. Never had an uh, incident in the history of this area. Would you mind going over the sequence of events once more? I'm sorry to ask this but we want to make sure we haven't left anything out. Maybe you'll remember something."

Emily glanced at Mark and he gave her the go-ahead sign. The kids crowded around Emily, and listened to every word as she recounted what happened.

She said, "In the minute I had to look in his eyes," she shuddered and straightened, "I'm almost positive he knows me. I never saw him before but something inside me says he thinks he knows me and...wants something from me." Emily shook her head. "Does that make sense?"

Notes taken, nothing further to discuss. The kitchen clock registered eight thirty. Two hours and fifteen minutes had passed since Pat died. When she finished, the officers thanked her again, and headed for the door. Emily followed them.

"Now what?" she said. "We want to see him. Where is he and how soon can we go there?"

The men exchanged glances. This was another difficult part of the job. "An autopsy has to be performed to determine cause of death."

Emily cried out, sickened with the reality of Pat sliced open, then stitched back together like making a doll. She hadn't pictured that gruesome procedure being performed on someone she loved. Movies and television cop shows depicted autopsies all the time. The sights and smells were discussed graphically. No secrets were kept from the coroner. Viewers learned more than they wanted to know about autopsies. Now that was part of her knowledge, another insult to Pat's body. As if being struck and killed by a car wasn't horrible enough.

"He must be found and pay for what he did. To all of us." And Emily broke down. Mark was there to comfort her. The family closed into a circle, everyone cried.

The policemen said they would advise the family as to when Pat could be seen and left.

Once she composed herself, Emily suggested that Mike take Mandy to the guest room and make sure she rested. He agreed and they left. Jake said he'd look around to see if any chores needed attention. He was restless and work was the solution. Meg went into the master bedroom to straighten up. Mark and Emily were alone.

"What can I do to help?"

He smoothed her long hair away from the face he'd loved for so many years. An intimate gesture without the sexual overtones of their last meeting.

"Pat and I were barely beginning to understand each other and now it's over. I don't know how I'll get through the next few days let alone the rest of my life."

Mark took her by the hand and led her to the living room. She was like a sleepwalker in need of direction before she got hurt. Emily curled up in a corner and hugged a soft brown velvet pillow. She closed her eyes and drifted. Mark covered her with a brown and beige throw blanket. He built a fire as he talked. Paper logs were already in place. All that was necessary was a match to ignite the fire. The scrape of a long match against the box caused Emily to shudder. The smell of sulfur faded with the flame, paper logs crackled and lit dry logs. "It's just a match, Emily. Nothing to be afraid of." He sat next to her, patted her shoulders, and massaged her thin neck.

"Friends will be stopping by. I told the caterer to bring an appropriate spread. That gives you time to rest, shower, and dress."

Emily murmured, "Thanks."

"I'll return at four to oversee, check the silver and keep a watchful eye. Jake said he'd help me. Are you listening?" She gave a weak nod. "The security alarm is off. I think it's too much for you and kids to be concerned with today. People will come and go this afternoon and evening. Is that all right with you?"

This time, Emily didn't respond. Mark kissed her soft cheek and went to search for Jake, Emily's fragrance on his lips.

He found Jake up in the exercise room. Weights and a workout bench were in a corner. Jake hefted two hundred pounds over his head, sinewy arms quivered at the top. Up and down, up and down, sweat poured from his face, dripped onto his chest. A final staggering effort finished the set, the weights dropped down and Jake dried hands and face with a towel. He sat, breathing hard, shoulders slumped.

"Pat and I worked together fixing up this room. He handed tools to me; we drank a few beers, and got to know each other. He was a good guy, ya know? Nuts about Mom. He would've turned himself inside out if she asked him to. Meg and I didn't like him at first but he kinda grew on us. Tough." Jake shook his head.

Mark looked around for a place to sit. He settled on the exercise bike. Perched high, he took in the surroundings. Strictly utilitarian. Except for an unusual painting, the walls were bare.

"This painting must be new. I haven't seen it before," Mark said.

"Mom's friend Lola is an artist. She told Mom she had a compulsion to paint it. She's a character. Ask Mom. It's an interesting story."

"I will. Emily wants to be a matchmaker."

"No way, Mark. You only have eyes for Mom. I noticed that a long time ago. Your secret's safe with me."

Mark was taken aback by the frankness in the young man. He was a diamond-in-the-rough guy, likeable and out-spoken.

"I didn't realize you were so perceptive. It's a good quality. I can see why Meg fell in love with you. I hoped she would have been interested in one of my sons but they were just friends. Remember what I said to you when you were engaged?"

"Yeah. How could I forget? You cornered me at the party and said 'take care of her or you'll answer to me'. That worried me for a long time."

"I meant it. After all, I am her Godfather But you can rest easy. I can tell that you and Meg are good together."

Relieved to hear he had Mark's approval, Jake picked up the weights to do another set.

"There is something on my mind," Mark said. Jake stopped in mid lift. "You and I have to become a team. Can I count on you to be there for your mother-in-law, no matter what comes up?"

Jake put the weights down and stuck out his big hand, roughened from years of working as carpenter. Mark met him halfway extending his manicured, smooth hand. A pact made in a gentlemen's agreement.

"That's a mean handshake you've got there, big fella."

"Yeah," said Jake, a grin on his rugged face.

"I'm leaving now so you're in charge. The alarm is off but the front door is locked. I want to find out what's being done to find that son-of-a-bitch. I'd like to see him strung up with his balls cut off." Mark's face was grim as he spoke, his jaw set in anger.

Jake laughed and couldn't stop.

"What the hell are you laughing at?"

"You. What you said about cutting his balls off. That's what cracked me up. I didn't know classy professors like you ever talked that way."

"Fuckin' A, big guy," said Mark.

And he offered up a high five to Jake. Their hands slapped together in mid air and Mark winced from Jake's power. They laughed some more. It was a relief from the events of the morning.

The doorbell rang rousing Emily from a deep slumber. She heard Tom's voice calling her through the intercom.

"Mom, open up."

Groggy, she made her way to the front door. Tom. She could see him through the peep hole. She heard Pat's voice in her head telling her to always verify the person at the door. He's watching over me, guiding me even though he's gone. Emily glanced at the alarm control box, noting it wasn't activated. Pat wouldn't like that one bit.

Emily opened the door and Tom scooped her into his arms. Julie was beside him, tears in her eyes. They looked as though they'd tumbled out of bed when she called from the hospital, threw a traveling bag together and rushed out the door. Tom's five o'clock shadow was out of control just as Emily envisioned, hair askew, dressed in clothes of questionable cleanliness, and the crisis had added a few lines to his almost thirty year old face.

"Thank God you're here," said Emily. She reached out to hug her daughter-in-law, Julie. "The last time you were here was the wedding."

"I bet you haven't eaten. I'll make breakfast for everyone." Checking his watch, he saw it was nearly noon. "I mean, brunch."

Julie took Emily's hand. "You look chilled, Mom. How about a nice hot bath? You can put on your favorite sweats and relax for a change."

Emily felt weak and let the kids look after her. Tired of responsibility, it was good to have them take over for her. Private thoughts had drained her.

"How can I turn them off?" Emily said.

"The bath?" Julie said.

"My thoughts," said Emily. "My mind is spinning round and round like a broken record. It won't stop." She put her hands out, palms up. "Make it stop, please." Face pale, hands trembling, "Can you unbreak my heart?"

Tom said, "Mom, do you have any valium in the house? That might take the edge off and let you cope better. Just for now."

Emily shook her head no. "I need some time and then I'll be okay." Her voice was flat, monotone. "Be here with me for a little while. Help me decide how to proceed. Friends are coming tonight to...I don't know. The police will let us know when we can see Pat. They're cutting him up now..."

She began to sink. Tom caught her before she fell.

"What can we do for her?" Julie said. "This is scary. Mom's always in control."

"When my Dad died, she was like this, but different. After all, Mom and Dad were married like forever and she met Pat a short time ago." Tom carried his mother to the couch in the living room. He covered her with the throw and placed a cushion under her head. "Julie, please get a wash cloth and ice for Mom then look around for Meg. The family's here somewhere." Julie did as he asked.

He stayed with his mom, spoke softly and rubbed her wrists. "Mom, we love you so much. We won't leave you alone. Don't be afraid, Mom. We'll take care of you."

He ran a hand through his unruly hair, tried not to cry. Satisfied that she slept, he went to the kitchen.

116

Emily dreamed of eyes staring, devouring her. What do you want from me? You're mine, the eyes seemed to say. I'm coming for you. In the dream the dark sky hung close to the beach. She couldn't find her way home. Meg's voice called and Emily woke up.

Meg had gone to the master bedroom an hour ago, saying she'd put things right before company came.

"I'm coming, Meg," she said as she hurried down the hall. "What's the matter?"

Meg sat cross-legged on tangled sheets in the middle of the bed, the room still in disorder.

"Mom, I'm so sorry but I haven't been honest with you for several months." Shining blond hair tumbled past her shoulders; amber eyes fringed with long lashes peered up at her Mom for understanding.

Emily climbed on the bed and sat cross-legged opposite Meg, the mirror image of each other.

"Tell me, honey. Whatever it is can't be that bad. In fact, nothing can be as bad as what happened today." Meg nodded.

"When Dad died, I was six weeks pregnant and whether it was from the shock of his sudden death or not, I had a miscarriage."

Emily recalled how terrible it was, one loss after the other.

"Jake and I having been trying to have another baby and now this."

She gestured to the robe thrown across the bed in haste to leave for their run this morning.

"And I got scared. Afraid a bad thing would happen to me again. We've had a lot of awful stuff, Mom." Meg choked back tears.

"But Mom, look at this." Meg pulled something out of her pocket. It was a shadowy black and white print. Emily reached for glasses always handy in a pocket or attached to a chain around her neck.

"What is it?"

"See that dot?" She pointed to a speck on the print. Next to the dot was an arrow with a sign. Emily could barely make out the word.

"Mom, it says baby. That dot is our baby."

117

"Oh my God. My little love." She folded Meg in her arms. "Thank you for telling me now. It's an unexpected gift. Just think. There will be two tiny cousins very close in age in the next eight months. How wonderful."

Emily's face lit up and she started to laugh. "This is dot baby and you're dot mom." Meg didn't get it. "Like a web site. WWW.dotmom."

"That's hilarious," said Meg and they laughed. A laugh tinged with sadness.

As Emily reached out to hug her daughter, her hand brushed against Pat's beige velour robe lying on the bed. Her fingers touched the lush sensual fabric, brushing it over and over. It felt warm, alive. She slipped the robe around her shoulders; her arms found the sleeves and put it on. She held it close, making herself part of the robe. Pat's robe, worn a few hours ago. It carried the cologne he favored, a musk scent guaranteed to excite her. Her body shook with the memories of countless pleasures.

Keening filled the air as she bent from the waist, rising up and down, up and down like a seesaw in rapid movement. Meg watched, mesmerized and frightened but she knew not to touch or interrupt her mother's grief.

Julie entered the room. She had been standing in the doorway and caught the tail end of the conversation and watched as Emily switched from joy to sorrow. Meg motioned for Julie to hush and wait. As quickly as it began, the mood left. Emily stopped the compulsive rocking and straightened up.

"It's like a tide washing over me, controlling, then releasing. Nothing I can do to stop it, but I'm not afraid and I don't want you to be. I'll be all right. I promise." Emily smiled at the girls.

"Julie," said Emily "do you have any baby news to share with us?"

Julie said, "Not ready yet. They all laughed, the spell was broken.

"Mom, first things first, is my motto. Tom sent me to gather the fold for one of his famous brunches."

"Tell him we'll be right there," said Emily over her shoulder. "I have to wash up."

Behind her, Julie got on the bed and whispered with Meg.

Girl stuff, thought Emily. We have to do some serious

bonding to survive, but a shower was next on her agenda. She removed the bloodied running jacket worn all morning and for the first time the rest of her blood stained clothes were revealed. She hugged herself as a shiver passed through her body. Her hands trembled as they pealed away the tee shirt and shorts, crushed them into a ball, and dumped the mess into a hamper. She faced the mirror. A haggard Emily looked back, a far cry from the youthful woman she'd been a few hours before. A reserve of strength welled up. "Okay lady, time to regroup," she said to the woman in the mirror. As she showered, she came up with a plan.

Dressed in clean clothes, wet hair wrapped in a towel, Emily followed tempting fragrances emanating from the kitchen. She was hungry and the family needed her to guide them.

Seated at the big table were the people she loved best, everyone taking portions from the platter of poached eggs, hash browns, and toast. Curls of steam rose from mugs of hot coffee and Tom had Emily's favorite food, orange sections and strawberries, arranged on a small plate.

After every morsel was consumed, Emily clinked her spoon against a mug for attention. All eyes turned to the head of the table.

"Listen up, gang. I've reached a decision as to the party, the funeral, and the next couple of days. Any suggestions or additions are welcome."

This was Emily at her best, in charge, making things happen. A collective sigh of relief came from the young people.

"Excuse me for interrupting Mom, but you don't have any credibility wearing that outfit," said Tom.

"What are you talking about?" said Emily.

"Tom," said Meg, making two syllables out of his one syllable name the way annoyed siblings do."That was so rude. Apologize to Mom."

He ignored his sister. "You came to the table wearing a towel on your head like some movie star from the forties. Joan Crawford or maybe Lana Turner. And while you're eating, the towel keeps slipping and now it's listing to portside like a drunken sailor. It's really funny. That's what I mean. No disrespect intended, Mom."

"Is he right?" Emily asked the group.

"Now that you mention it, yes, it's kind of funny," said Mandy.

"Does everyone agree?" They all agreed.

"Okay gang, the towel comes off and no matter what I look like, I'm still the boss," said Emily. "Later the caterer is coming. If you need a change of clothes, and I think you will, please go shopping in my closet and Pat's. He won't mind." Mandy gasped. "Sorry honey, but sometimes a sense of humor is the only thing that carries you through bad times. It's okay to laugh. Our hearts are broken, the sadness too much to bear, but it's okay to laugh."

"Excuse me, Mom," said Meg, but Jake and I will go home for clothes. Nothing here could fit Jake and I'll be more comfortable in my own clothes. Thanks anyway."

Amanda raised a tentative hand. "Mike and I will do the same and we can bring a change for you guys," indicating Tom and Julie, "if you want."

"Thanks," said Julie. "We packed enough for overnight so we're cool. We'll hang with Mom for the afternoon."

Emily looked around the table, pleased that the kids spoke up and continued. "Next, I think friend will drop by this evening out of respect. I want the exercise room locked. It has my martial arts equipment and charts displayed and that's personal.

"Why, Mom?" said Mike. "I agree with you but I'm curious."

"Pat wanted me to become good at martial arts and most of all, he wanted me to be able to protect myself. From what, I don't know. But it's been a challenging skill to learn and now I'm learning how to disable an attacker and then run like hell, screaming all the way. When we have time and no one is around, I'll show you what the Sensei has the patience to teach me. He's the Master at the Dojo.

"Tonight will be like a wake. We'll eat, drink, and talk about happy times with Pat. He and I discussed burial and we both left instructions for cremation. He wants his ashes to be scattered, some over the ocean by plane, and if any of you would like some to keep, you can take as much as you want."

"I took my Dad all over the world in little pill bottles during my traveling days," Tom said. "He kept me company on long trips and I really felt his presence. I still have some." He looked at the family seated around the table. "It worked for me."

Emily consulted her list. "There won't be a funeral. I think a memorial service would be appropriate, if that's all right with Mandy." Mandy nodded. "We can hold it here on Monday. That will give me time to notify his business associates and anyone else you can think of.

We'll go see him together when the police say we can. That should be tomorrow. After that, it's just us chickens and please everyone, let's stay loving and close all our lives. This family is growing and will continue to grow."

Meg raised a glass of juice."A toast to our family, our beloved Pat, and to new little people growing as we speak."

Glasses and mugs lifted, touched, and brunch was over.

Tom searched Pat's closet. Just curious about the man Mom married. A scent of musk after shave permeated the enclosed room. Clothes hung two inches apart facing left like soldiers at attention. No parade rest here. The atmosphere was charged with expectancy, as if awaiting orders.

"A lot of suits in here, big guy, and something else. It's like Testosterone Central. Very masculine. Just like Pat." He called to Jake who just returned from a trip home for a change of clothes. "Nothing that'll fit you. Maybe a cuff link. Pat dressed in what you might call powerful, yet conservative. Not my style."

"Yeah, little brother. You like the baggy pants, fancy shirts, and a long scarf wrapped around your neck."

Tom laughed at his brother-in-law.

"I'd never wear stuff like that even if you paid me," said Jake.

Tom's foot struck something sharp at the back of the closet.

"What the hell?" he said, with a grunt of pain.

He bent down and found a metal box. About one foot square in size, a big lock in place. He carried it out and placed it on the bed.

"Mom," Tom said as Emily entered the room, "what's this? Must be something important."

Emily touched the box."I've never seen it before. Jake, would you get Pat's key ring? It's in his middle office drawer."

Jake returned with the keys. She examined them, some she'd never noticed before. She found the key for the big lock and opened it.

"I'm too nervous to lift the lid," said Emily to her son and son-in-law. "I feel as if I've invaded Pat's confidential information."

"I understand," said Tom, "but his will may be in there, or something that concerns you." Emily didn't stir. She was lost in thought.

"Here goes nothing," said Tom as he lifted the lid. He and Emily

121

peered into the box. Jake moved closer to get a look.

"A book with another lock," said Jake. "He was really weird about security, wasn't he?"

Tom elbowed his brother-in-law, giving him a shut-your-face look and laughed in an attempt to lighten the mood.

"Prying secrets from the box, take two," he said as he found a tiny key and opened the book. "It's a journal, Mom. Okay if we read it?"

"No. I better do it," she said with hands clenched so tight the knuckles showed white.

"The first entry was about twelve years ago." She looked up at the boys, a frown on her face. "Pat's wife died somewhere in that time frame." She skimmed through the pages, confused and upset at reading his inner thoughts. A page jumped out at her. It was dated the night they'd met. On full alert, she read aloud.

"Met THE woman tonight after a ten year search." She glanced at the boys. This was so strange. "That's the night we met." She took a deep breath and continued. "She is perfect for me. Will protect her from harm for the rest of my life. A promise I intend to keep."

"That's all?" said Jake.

"That's all he wrote on this page."

She sighed. How well she remembered the night they met. Now she was a widow. Again. She turned another page. Blank. The next page was full, writing cramped, recent dates. She shut the diary.

"That's more than enough right now. I've got my hands full."

"What does it mean?" said Tom.

"It means there were facets to Pat that will never be revealed. It means I could ponder over his words for a lifetime and never know the truth."

The young men listened to her, the question of what the journal was about unspoken for now.

"It means I should lock it up and deal with it another less emotional time." She placed her hands on their hands. "We'll move on with our lives and not look in the rear view mirror too often."

Emily handled the locked box as if it contained a precious gem and placed it on a shelf in her closet.

"Take anything you want, Tom, and shut the door when you're through. I love you both. Just thought I'd mention that." She left the room.

In silence, the boys watched her leave not knowing what they'd witnessed.

"What was that all about? Do you have a clue?" said Jake.

"Not a clue." More silence.

"Mom's tough," said Jake.

"Yeah, she is," said Tom. He glanced around the room one more time and left the room empty handed.

Door chimes rang incessantly by four o'clock. The caterer and her assistant made a multitude of trips carting food, tables, and sundries needed for the wake. They took over the kitchen as they stirred, chopped, steamed, doing chef chores. A cleaned-up Tom sat on a bar stool in the corner and observed while taking mental notes. He loved to cook so it was a bonus to watch experts at work. Soon mouth watering aromas wafted through the air. The scent of mushrooms, onions and slivers of chicken simmering in broth warmed the atmosphere in the house of mourning.

Mark Wagner arrived to oversee the proceedings as promised. Once he was convinced all would go smoothly, he asked Tom to gather Emily and the family for a meeting in the living room.

They assembled almost with reluctance, sure that Mark must have an update from the police. Mark admired the way everyone had rallied. Emily wore a long black silk skirt with a black high neck sweater, her only adornment a heavy gold chain, hair swept back away from the classic thin face. Makeup didn't quite conceal shadows under her eyes giving her a haunted look. When all were settled, some on couches, some on the floor, Mark leaned against the wall next to the fireplace. His sandy brown hair was still damp from the shower. He wore a navy blue suit, pale blue shirt, with his tie loose at the neck. Removing his glasses, he cleared his throat and began.

"You can see Pat tomorrow anytime after eleven. I took the liberty of arranging for Griffith's Funeral Parlor to pick him up. The coroner suggested it would be better for you to go there rather than to his domain. Personally I agree with his judgment. Emily, is that all right with you?" Emily blinked her eyes, and then mouthed a silent yes.

"About evidence." All eyes on Mark. Tension in the room was palpable. "Tire tracks of a dune buggy were found before the tide came in. Parked behind a dune where you said you saw a man, all the way south down to where the incident happened. Paint fragments were found on Pat's clothing. Only fragments and with the salt water, who knows how they can trace it. There's a bulletin out for a blue dune buggy, scratched surface. Good work, fast for this small town. And O'Keefe is on the case full time."

A collective gasp and harsh, bitter words erupted from the family.

"This family is as dear to me as my own. Meg and Tom, I've known you since before you were born. Know that I will clear my calendar for the next few weeks and be available in any capacity. Any questions?"

"Cause of death?" said Jake.

"Massive injuries sustained when his head hit the trunk of the car. If it brings any comfort to you, he died instantly. The impact was sudden and he probably wasn't aware of the accident for more than a moment."

Mandy ran from the room sobbing. Mike hurried to catch up.

Chimes rang out. Emily was nearest the door. She looked through the viewer, saw a flower display and heard a voice call out, "Delivery." Emily opened the door. A young man handed over the huge bouquet and stood there waiting. Tom was the first to reach her.

"Mom, how nice." He took the bouquet and handed the driver a dollar. "Let's see who sent them." He handed the little white envelope to Emily who looked at it and let it drop to the flagstone floor.

Mark made his way through the kids, grasped Emily by the arm, retrieved the note and escorted her back to the living room.

"What's wrong, Emily? Someone sent you flowers and what?"

"I don't know. Too many flowers in one bouquet all kind of squashed together. It's too extravagant and tasteless. I don't know people like that."

"Open the card."

She did. In a cramped handwriting, words jumped out. *Flowers for my Goddess*. She handed the card to Mark. "It's the man from the beach. I know it."

"I'll call O'Keefe. Anything else?"

"Help me get through this. All of this." Expressive hands gestured in an appeal, the wedding band twisted on her finger. "Yes, I would like privacy. Ask the kids to tidy up, please. Company is coming." Mark headed for the door. "Mark." He stopped. "Thanks for everything."

He turned and left Emily alone.

Lost in thought, she didn't hear the chimes, hadn't noticed two hours passed until sounds at the door roused her from reverie. Company had arrived. Emily rose to greet her guests.

Not invited to the gathering, Clifford Lansdale shambled along the beach with binoculars dangling from his neck. Wired on too much caffeine, Vicodin pain killer warring with his screwed up system, he moved on. Hard to find a good vantage point to watch. Beach cops patrolling everywhere. What's a decent citizen to do? All I need is one good peek at my Goddess. And one good touch, a feel, a smell. Yes. His body heated in dark places in spite of the chill wind blowing off the ocean. He whispered to the wind, "Patrick Corwin fell off the wall, Patrick Corwin had a great fall. All the King's horses and all the King's men couldn't put Patrick Corwin together again."

And there she was, his beauty, in full view of the beach. Dressed in black. Black as the night. He dropped to his knees behind tall pampas grass in the high dunes and snapped pictures before she turned away. Satisfied for now, Clifford Lansdale began the long walk back to his mansion. Dune buggy out of commission for now.

Gazing out at the beach, lost in thought, Emily suddenly had the shivers. For no apparent reason, she sensed someone out in the darkness, watched her. She hurried away from the sliding glass door to where she felt safer.

Two by two, like Noah's Ark, friends came to the door. At first, Emily was there to welcome them but Mark interceded and appointed Tom and Julie to that task. He wanted the widow seated in the living room and the guests to come to her. Emily was too numb to argue, grateful he was in charge. Elegant in black, holding on as best she could, she sat while the family took over the hospitality. A stack of CD's provided music from the Beatles up to the latest hits as background to what otherwise might have been a somber scene. A fire crackled, casting shadows and light as friends mingled, sampling hors d' oeuvres and cocktails served by two waiters.

A crystal vase filled with fragrant flowers was flanked by silver candlesticks on the sideboard. A beautiful setting for a tragic occasion. Pictures of Pat were on the mantel. Pat and his daughter; running with Emily; riding his treasured motorcycle wearing leathers and helmet; Pat alive and well.

Emily got up and wandered about. Friends, two by two, everyone partnered. She was on the outside looking in. How would she begin again, she wondered It was a bitter pill the last time. The sadness of being alone, no companion to accompany her after being married most of her life. How thrilled she was to meet him. How promising their future had looked. Her mind was like a twisting kaleidoscope shifting memories of her life. She smiled, accepted sympathy and hugs from a distance, an outsider in her home.

Mark touched her shoulder. "Lola's here." Startled, Emily turned and there she was. Stunning Lola-not looking so stunning at the moment- makeup streaked from tears shed on the trip from Jacksonville. The women touched hands, an eloquent unspoken dialogue between them.

"If I start talking now, I'll cry and not be able to stop. Please understand. And thank you for driving all the way down. You've met Mark. He's the catch I told you about."

Mark caressed Emily's face with a gentleness displaying his feelings for her. Lola didn't miss the gesture and mentally crossed Mark Wagner off her list of eligible men.

"Emily, I'll take care of myself. I want to see your kids, have a drink, and taste the goodies."

Emily moved in close to Lola and whispered in her ear. "Stop in my bathroom and paint a new face for yourself. Your tears did some damage."

"Thanks for the warning. There are no words to express how I feel about your loss. You and Pat..." She stopped. There were no words.

Emily said, "Later, when everyone leaves, I have a question about the painting you gave me. We'll go upstairs and look at it. Okay?"

"Of course," and she left to repair her face and to find Tom, her favorite.

Mark was at Emily's side during the brief exchange with Lola.

"Is she someone you could be interested in?"

"Give it a rest. Introduce me to your other friends. I'd like to meet them."

"Oh, sorry," said Emily, embarrassed she forgot Mark didn't know this crowd.

The evening passed; food was consumed, the ice melted, candles burned down, the fire was merely an ember and energy flagged. There were tearful goodbyes at the door. It was a good wake.

The last of the guests departed except for Lola who had spent the night hanging out with the young people. Meg and Amanda were asleep, the boys ready to pack it in. The caterers finished cleaning and left. Strains of 'The Party's Over' came through the speakers. It wasn't a party, thought Emily, but it was over and for her, just a beginning.

Lola showed up, coat on, bag over a shoulder, ready to get on the road.

"Not so fast," said Emily. "The painting, remember? Follow me."

"All right if I tag along?" said Mark.

Somehow he still looked fresh, buttoned down, not at all rumpled. How does he do that? Emily wondered. She took his hand and the three of them went to the back of the house, up the stairs where Emily unlocked the door to her room. She turned the lights on and made her way to the painting.

"So?" Lola said. "What's your question about my masterpiece?"

Mark admired the painting once more, impressed with the artist's work.

"Do you have precognition, Lola? Don't laugh. This is a serious question."

"What do you mean?"

"Look." She pointed to the canvas. "There are three shadowy male figures behind me. You said I'm The Emerging Woman, right?"

"Definitely."

Mark listened with interest to the women, not knowing where this was going.

"You didn't know my first husband, but this figure resembles him." Emily indicated the shape she referred to.

Mark moved in to examine the shape. "Yes," he said. "It does, in an impressionistic way."

"This second figure is close to an image of Pat. See?"

Both Lola and Mark leaned toward the painting and scrutinized the figure. They agreed there was a likeness to Pat.

Lola shrugged her shoulders. "So what are you driving at, Emily? I painted whatever I was compelled to. Remember I told you that it really painted itself."

"Don't you see?" Emily was nearly frantic. "Larry is dead. Now Pat is dead." A trembling finger touched the third figure and pulled back as if burned. "Who is this?"

Emily's cry pierced the air breaking the tension. Holding back all evening had been too much for her. The calm facade crumbled, she had no need to restrain herself anymore. Mark cradled her in his arms, stroking hair loosened from the clip holding it in place. He made

127

soothing, reassuring sounds as he led her down the stairs. Lola turned out the lights and followed them.

When they reached the house, Lola said, "I don't know who that is or if it's anything but my imagination. All I did was paint. I have no mystical powers I'm aware of and I don't have a crystal ball to look into the future. It's a coincidence, that's all." She hugged Emily who still cried little sobs. "I like your friend Mark but he's not my type." She smiled. Emily stopped crying and grinned at her.

"You're a goof. Drive carefully please."

"You're both goofs," said Mark. "And very interesting goofs, at that."

They watched her drive away. A full moon shone amidst a myriad of stars. Gnarled cypress trees lining the driveway were highlighted by moonlight. They looked like huge sentinels guarding the house.

"Time to go. I'll call after I talk to the police tomorrow. Get some sleep."

He turned to leave and paused. Emily looked fragile, framed in the doorway by the large oak doors. "You're not alone. You have the children and you have me."

"Thanks, Mark. Good night." She reached up and kissed his cheek.

He waited until she went inside and closed the door before he left.

Inside, Emily stood before the key pad. Her finger hit #1013 and the on button. A red light illuminated the pad casting a glow. Mesmerized by the light, Emily drew near as a moth to the flame. She saw the eyes of evil in the red shine, the eyes of the man on the beach. Her eyes squeezed tight to block the image. She breathed deeply forcing herself to look again. Overtired, she imagined danger wherever she turned turn. Get to bed. No more bogeyman tonight. With caution, she placed one foot in front of the other and made her solitary way down the hall.

"Thank you, Meg," whispered Emily as she entered the bedroom she left in total disarray and now was in order. Her daughter had cleaned up as she said she would. "What a girl." Emily spoke softly and kept herself company on this first night alone. It was a comfort the children were there but they wouldn't remain. Past experience taught her she'd be all right in the long run. Many long runs ahead. That's what I do. I coach, I run, and now I'm almost ready for whatever lies ahead. Clothes put away, she reached for a nightgown and changed her mind. Pajamas for now, no need to look sexy.

Sad, so sad, Emily crept under the white quilt and pulled it to her chin. The thrashing began. She couldn't get comfortable. The bed was cold. It never used to be so cold. Rolling over to Pat's side, she caught his scent on the pillow, on the sheets, everywhere. Torture, this was torture. She sat up, turned on the lamp, and searched around the room. It was on the chair, Pat's velour robe. She crawled out of bed, slipped into the robe, grabbed his pillow and a blanket. Emily opened Pat's closet, made a nest on the floor and snuggled up. Compulsive order in the enclosed space had a calming effect, driving away the chaos in her mind.

Chapter 22

"Mom, wake up." Meg kneeled next to her mom, still asleep on the closet floor. "How come you're in here?" She brushed Emily's hair back, examined her face for signs of wear and tear. "Mom?"

Emily opened one eye and groaned. She smiled at her lovely daughter. "What time is it?"

"Nine o'clock. Uncle Mark called to say he's on the way with breakfast. Doesn't he ever sleep?"

Emily sat up in a rush, gathered bedding from the floor. She threw everything on the neatly made up bed and hurried to the bathroom.

"He'll look perfect and I look like something the cat dragged in." She called to Meg, "Do you think I should wear black?"

"Black is good but it makes you look even thinner than you are. How about your gray jersey dress and a silk scarf? I love you in that. How come you slept in the closet? I straightened your bed, did you notice? The sheets were all tangled. It looked like you fought with someone and lost."

"I couldn't sleep there. I don't know why I went into Pat's closet but I did and finally dozed off."

Emily entered the bedroom wrapped in a towel. "Honey, please take the dress and scarf out while I put on makeup. My refection in the mirror is scary. I'll need a different cream for every inch of my face and a pound of foundation and blush to give me a natural look."

"Mom, I checked you out when you were asleep and you looked pretty good. Don't worry about it. Today you'll be with everyone who loves you." Meg moved close. "This is kind of like when Dad died. No warning. All of a sudden he's gone and nothing is the same. Poor Mandy." Tears spilled down her cheeks. "I'll be a good sister to her."

Emily hugged her daughter. She didn't want to cry this morning. Time for that later. Right now, there was too much to do.

Starting Over

The door chimes rang. "Honey, get the door please. Don't let anyone in until you look through the peep hole. Be sure to disengage the alarm before the door is opened. Hit 1-0-1-3, then OFF."

Emily handed a tissue to her and Meg left while she dressed. The makeup job would have to be quick.

Voices in the kitchen told Emily everyone was up as she zipped the dress, tied a scarf around her neck, slipped on pumps, and headed in that direction. Freshly brewed coffee got her salivary glands working. Shows you how a few hours of sleep can restore a semblance of health, she thought. Even the movie projector in her brain stopped giving her a respite from the recording of the accident that played an endless loop. She knew it would begin again. Better eat while she could.

Mark leaned against the far wall of the kitchen near the window, arms crossed in front in a casual attitude. He looked like an ad from a fashion magazine, dressed in a gray light wool jacket over a white shirt and black pleated trousers. Black suede loafers completed the picture. Country gentleman at home. He appeared relaxed but Emily knew him so well. He was on full alert all the time, no detail escaped him.

Seated around the big table, the kids helped themselves to bagels, cream cheese and jelly and Nova Scotia lox, subdued conversation in progress.

Emily paused in the doorway. A new recording began. Good images this time. A fierce protective feeling filled her. This is my family. To hell with anyone who harms them. Do you hear me up there? Watch over these dear people. Please.

"Hi gang."

Everyone broke stride for an instant, forks in mid-air, bagels in mid-bite, coffee mugs in mid-destination. A chorus of 'Mom, it's about time you woke up.', 'I like that dress.', 'Have some breakfast. It's delicious.'. Mark pulled a chair out for Emily. Meg poured coffee.

"Good morning." Emily touched Mark's hand in greeting. "You're my favorite caterer. Thanks. By the way, last night was supposed to be simple fare. Out of control, hmm?" He nodded

She sat, a steaming mug in hand, nibbled on half a bagel spread with a light coat of marmalade. Meg pushed a plate with sliced navel oranges and strawberries toward her. "Thanks, honey," she said, and bit into a juicy strawberry. A drop of juice dripped on her hand. She wiped it with a napkin. The stain looked like blood. A shiver went through her. She pushed the plate away and left the table. Coffee mug in hand, she crossed to the glass slider and pressed her forehead to the cool glass.

"What is it?" Mark's voice low so the kids couldn't hear.

She shook her head, choking with emotion. "The strawberry juice made a stain like blood," she said. He patted her arm and his warmth soothed her. "The weather's bleak today. Yesterday, the sun was shining. Will it ever shine again?"

"We're survivors, my dear. Time will heal us but we never forget."

He turned to watch the kids. "When breakfast's finished, I have some information."

Here it comes, she thought. Here comes the bad part.

Tom directed traffic for the clean-up and when the kitchen was in order, he said what they all wanted to say. "Now what?"

"Let's get comfortable in the family room while I fill you in."

No one could get comfortable. They sat at the edges of the couch, the chairs, leaned against walls, in anticipation. Mark had their undivided attention.

Mark said,"Mr. Griffith from the funeral home called. We can go there any time after twelve o'clock. He said the newspaper called yesterday regarding a notice to be in this morning's edition, so he gave them a time for visitation. Two to four o'clock today. I didn't know he would do that without family approval but he did. Trying to be helpful. He said that flower arrangements were arriving all morning. I hope this doesn't upset you anymore than you are already. A lot of people want to pay respect to Pat and to all of you."

Emily sat motionless, hands folded in her lap, head bowed. The family waited to see her reaction. They would respond in kind.

"It's the right thing to do," said Emily. "Funeral protocol. Okay. But if it wasn't okay, it's too late to change so we're committed. We can't turn friends away at the door."

A collective sigh of relief and everyone spoke at once. "What should I wear?", "How soon do we leave?", and "Is that all for now, Uncle Mark?"

"That's all for now," said Mark. "We'll leave at twelve fifteen. It's thirty minutes south of here. We'll take two cars, mine seats four. Emily, does this meet with your approval?"

She forced a wan smile and nodded, grateful once again he took charge. She knew she was incapable of making a decision. Meg had to tell her what to wear.

"Go shopping in my closet," said Emily. "Don't ask permission to wear anything. You have carte blanche."

Everyone dispersed, leaving Emily and Mark alone in the family room.

"Come for a walk with me," said Emily as she rose and took his hand. "I need some fresh air."

Together they left the house. Emily breathed deeply, filling her lungs with warm moist air. She would get through this nightmare, she was sure of that.

Linking arms with Mark, she set the pace in spite of wearing two inch heels. She wanted to move, to feel alive. Mark held her capable hand.

"Want to race?" he said.

She grinned. "When this is over, we will. I promise. But I warn you, I'm very fast."

"Sounds like a challenge to me."

"It is," she said and walked faster. "Thanks again. I feel a bit more human today. Maybe it's because I had a few good hours of sleep but more because you were here each time I needed you." She squeezed his hand and they headed back.

The kids were in various stages of dressing when Emily called for a meeting in the master bedroom. A cardboard box labeled photographs and memorabilia was on the bed. They straggled in, buckling belts, tying ties, brushing hair. Emily's heart filled with love at the sight of them.

"What's up, Mom?" said Tom.

"Remember when your Dad died, each of us selected snapshots and his favorite cookies and snacks for him to take on the journey?"

"And his floppy hat," said Meg with a wistful smile.

"Don't forget the old golf ball, 'cause we knew he wouldn't want a new one," said Tom. Emily smiled.

"I'd like to do the same for Pat. This box contains tangible memories he collected over the years. I planned to put the snaps in an album but ran out of time." Emily stopped. There was the bad choice of words again. Ran out of time. That's exactly what happened. Pat ran out of time. Oh, dear God. Time is so precious. She must remember not to waste any of it.

"Mom, are you still here?" Meg called.

"Yes. I was thinking how important it is to live life to the fullest. Try to make each day count. Now enough of philosophizing. Mandy, look through the box and find memories your Dad treasured enough to take along."

"Okay, Mom."

She opened the box, and sifted through the stack. Mike hovered over her. She made room for him to sit and help her with selections.

"Finish dressing guys, and be thinking about other items that might be included. We have to leave in about half an hour."

"A Frank Sinatra CD?" said Tom as he left the room.

"Good," said Emily. "Jerry Mulligan, too. He loved jazz, didn't he, Mandy."

"Loved it," she said. A small pile of photos grew next to her. "May I keep some of these?"

"Of course. Take as many as you want."

Jake came in holding a hat. "What about this, Mom?" Pat's special running hat.

"Excellent choice," said Emily. "Who knows? There might be a running track where he's going and he'll need his hat."

When everyone dressed and brought their choices for Emily's approval, it was time to leave. Mark had spent the past hour on the phone. She was aware of his intense voice coming from the kitchen desk area the whole time she'd been occupied with her task. Now he was the most important person in her life next to her children.

He appeared in the doorway, calm and unruffled. "All aboard," he said.

Emily told Tom to put the journal back in the case. "That's not going with Pat. Lock the cabinet and bring me the key, wise guy."

Tom hurried and returned a few minutes later with the key and two CD's. "Can we take some decent music along? Funeral homes have the worst music. They always sound like you're at a funeral."

"Well?" they all said in unison.

"Good idea," said Emily. "Pick some we'd like and let's go."

Emily activated the alarm as everyone piled into the cars. The red light gave the ominous shine that never failed to make Emily shudder. She slammed the big oak door and set the alarm. Again the warm clean air felt good. Mark waited at the car, passenger door open. She got in and fastened the safety belt as the car shifted through gears down the road, made a right and another right toward I 95. It was time to see Pat.

Chapter 23

Bluest of blue sky, no clouds to be seen, not a day for a funeral, was on Emily's mind as the cars headed north. Mark pulled into a circular driveway and parked in front of Griffith's Funeral Home. A tall well-dressed man in a dark suit moved through carved doors and down the steps, arriving at the car as it stopped. Like an actor waiting in the wings for his cue, performance flawless. She remembered him well. The undertaker she'd used for Larry, excellent in his job. Mark had his wife's funeral here.

Andrew Griffith extended a hand to Emily and helped her out of the car. "Mrs. Corwin. My sympathy to you and your family."

"Thank you."

Mark hurried over as he signaled Mike to escort Mandy from the car.

"Andrew," said Mark as he approached him, hand held out in greeting.

"Mark." The men shook hands.

Emily introduced Mandy and Mike to Mr. Griffith and to the other kids as they climbed the stairs.

"Where is my husband?"

"Follow me."

In a manner worthy of royalty, Mr. Thompson led the procession down a wine red carpeted hall past several closed doors. Classical music poured from the sound system, nothing charged with emotion, strings, pianos, and harps. Emily felt sick. She turned to find Tom at her elbow with his selection of CD's. She gestured for him to speak to the funeral director.

"I will soon, Mom. Let's see Pat first." He took her arm as if he could shield his mother for what came next.

At the end of the long hall stood an easel with a sign saying Patrick Corwin. The double doors were closed.

Mark stepped in front."I'll take it from here, Andrew. Thank you for your consideration on short notice."

The quiet man nodded and backed away.

Mark faced the family. "We are making the best we can of a tragedy. The Griffith's accommodated my request for privacy. No one will disturb us for an hour. Afterward the room will be open for visitors. If members of the press come in looking for comments or interviews, please send them to me. This is important. The less said the better. Ready?"

They responded with nods and entered the room.

Surrounded by a garden of flower bouquets, the coffin was set on a raised platform. White tapers in brass candlesticks flickered in the dim light. Emily made her way with a pounding heart. She gazed down at her husband. Deep breaths. The peaceful look people speak of was there, painted with skill on his dead face. She knew he would have no peace until the man responsible paid for his crime. She knew that somewhere Pat raged. An eye for an eye raced through her mind. The endless loop began.

She whispered to him, "I promise he'll pay. I'll make him pay." She beckoned the kids to join her. "We have gifts for you." She placed a wedding snapshot in the coffin. Her eyes sought Mark at the back of the group. "I know you selected his blue suit. Thank you."

Emily moved to the side allowing the family to close in and leave tokens they had selected.

Frank Sinatra's voice filled the air. It was a relief to break the heavy somber atmosphere. The kids moved around the room, looked at flowers, noted cards from the senders, and talked to one another.

A commotion at the door drew everyone's attention. Andrew Griffith attempted to prevent a man from entering. Mark hurried to see who the intruder was. He wanted to avoid any unpleasantness. Emily gasped in astonishment. She ran to the door, arms wide open to embrace the newcomer.

"How did you know?" she said.

The tall man scooped her up and cradled her in his arms. Tears streamed from his eyes.

"Hush, little one."

He spoke in heavily accented English; a flavor of the Middle

East predominated. When Emily's tears subsided he set her down. A black ribbon was pinned over his heart, an embroidered black velvet yarmulke on his graying hair.

"This is Samuel, Pat's close friend from Israel. I met him on our honeymoon," she told her family.

Samuel walked past everyone, headed straight for the coffin. Bowing his head, he chanted a prayer in Hebrew. Then he withdrew a small knife from his pocket and slashed the black ribbon. He closed the knife, pocketed it and turned to the family who watched with rapt attention.

"I am Samuel Levy. A better friend than Pat, I have never had. He was another son to me. Bill Hays from corporate office phoned giving to me the saddest of information. Shalom."

He walked to each of the kids, embracing them in bear hugs, and planted a kiss on each cheek. When he stood in front of Jake who towered over the gathering, he extended his hand.

Tom, never one to be shy, was full of questions. "How did you get here so fast?"

"I have available to me a Gulfstream V anytime day or night," said Samuel, a flash of humor in his black eyes. "We will talk more on this subject but first I want to know how such a terrible accident happened to my friend."

Emily took Samuel's hand, and led him to Mark who stayed in the background observing the extraordinary interruption.

"This is my best friend, Mark Wagner. He's been by my side since yesterday morning. If it's all right with you, Mark, would you answer Samuel's questions?"

"Of course," said Mark.

The men shook hands and sat down at the back of the chapel. When their conversation ended, Samuel returned.

"How long are you staying?" Emily said.

"One hour."

"Why so soon?"

"Business."

"You came all this way to see Patrick."

"Yes. And you also."

Emily was overwhelmed. A very long trip to pay homage to a friend. Pat would have loved this. Are you here, Pat? Can you see us? Fleeting thoughts from her fragmented mind.

"Tell us about the ribbon you're wearing. It must be a custom for mourning," Tom said.

"Yes. The ribbon signifies the death of a loved one. A family member. Most everyone lost parts of families in the camps and when my son Yehuda and Pat became close friends, we adopted Pat as a brother. The ribbon is worn over the heart and slashed to show the pain of loss. It is what you say, tearing your heart out."

Mandy came over and tugged at Samuel's hand. "Do you remember me? I'm Amanda, Pat's daughter."

Samuel looked at the heart shaped face, a few freckles scattered over her cheeks, short light brown hair tousled from running fingers through too many times.

"Yes, my dear."

Emily beckoned to Samuel and they moved to a private corner of the large room. She leaned close to him, not knowing quite how to ask what might be a delicate question. Heavy lidded eyes filled with the sorrow of centuries gazed down at her. She watched his eyes widen in recognition before she spoke. A scarred finger touched his closed mouth and touched hers and he gave an almost imperceptible shake of the great head.

"No" he said without words, "never". He lifted her hand and kissed it with a delicate brush of his lips. She had asked him what the journal meant, was Pat a spy or did he do anything illegal. Samuel closed up. She would never know. Maybe the journal would have some meaning but probably not. Later. When the family left.

It was almost two o'clock. The Israeli stood up and bid Shalom to the family. He hugged Emily, placing hands on her slender shoulders and kissed first one cheek, then the other, whispered, "An eye for an eye." The words swirled in Emily's head. She nodded. He exited as swiftly as he entered leaving a subtle change in the air.

Visitation hours began.

Many friends wore sunglasses inside the chapel. So did Clifford Lansdale. Dressed up in casual business attire as if he were an associate of the deceased, he entered the large room. His Goddess, so beautiful in gray, sat quiet and still facing the coffin. He squinted to catch a glimpse of his handiwork. All patched up are you, Patrick? Nice salon they have going here. Now was the chance to touch her hand if only for a moment. He strode over, new name in mind, and offered his hand along with sympathy.

"Mrs. Corwin, I'm so sorry for your loss. Patrick was a good man, He will be missed. Jerry Field from the office."

Emily glanced up to see the man with sunglasses speaking to her. Automatically she extended her hand and he held hers just a bit longer than anyone else had all afternoon. What did he say his name was? Jerry Field? Patrick never mentioned such a person. He moved on and she spoke to the next friend.

Outside, Clifford wanted to dance, shout, run wild. Instead he walked to his silver Mercedes parked toward the back and went home. Her hand carried a scent of heaven and he wanted her. Soon, dearest Goddess. Soon.

At four o'clock, the last few visitors left as Andrew Griffith entered the room. Mark signaled for him to shut the doors. The kids said their final farewells to Pat and they moved at a slow pace, pausing every few step to look back at him. A painful procession. Not a dry eye among them. Even Jake, who prided himself on being the strong silent type, had to be comforted by Meg.

Emily stood alone, close to the coffin. "Goodbye, my darling. We'll get to know each other in a better world." She plucked a white hibiscus from a garland and placed it on his hands. "I love you," she whispered and hurried away, not glancing back. As she left the room, she heard the final click as the latch closed on the coffin.

Her family waited outside in the dismal afternoon. Billowing black clouds obscured the sun visible when they entered the chapel several hours earlier. A threat of rain was present. The weather suited the mood.

"Let's go home, have a hot meal, relax for a while and then it'll be time for you to leave for your own homes," said Emily.

She headed to the waiting car, Mark at the wheel.

"That's Mom," Meg said. "She's ready to work on life as a single person again and she needs space to figure out how to do it."

"I don't like it," Tom said, "but I respect her need to be alone."

At home, the answer phone light blinked. Emily listened to the message and turned to the expectant faces. "Mr. Griffith said the ashes would be delivered Tuesday. Maybe next weekend you could come over and help yourself to whatever you'd like, within reason of course. No furniture or paintings included in the offer." The last remark brought a touch of humor to the grim young faces.

A fire burned, the smell of hickory mingled with roasted chicken Mark warmed in the range. A scent of apple pie combined to tempt the appetites.

"I didn't think food would appeal to me but I admit to being very hungry," Tom said. "Let's hear it for our personal caterer, Uncle Mark."

A few chuckles and quiet applause followed. The guys set the dining room table, the girls cut up a mixed green salad, and dinner was ready. Emily came in the kitchen. She wore blue jeans and an old pink cotton shirt. Her hair, brushed until it shone, tied up in a pony tail. A touch of blusher enhanced the pale cheeks and gave Emily a subtle glow she didn't feel.

"Mom, you look so pretty." Mandy said.

"I don't feel pretty It's an illusion but if I appear well, perhaps in time I'll feel well. Thanks, honey. Before we dine, please someone set a place for Pat."

A gasp of astonishment from the gang at this peculiar request.

"I realize you think poor Mom's lost it." All heads bobbed up and down. "Trust me. I cannot dismiss his life so quickly. He was taken from us in an instant and I need time to separate his being here from not being here. Indulge me, please."

Mark interjected. "I'm leaving now. I'll stay close to your Mom. I couldn't have survived without her help when my Laurie died. She knows I am a call away. She'll probably get tired of my attention." He looked at Emily. "I promise not to be intrusive."

She took his arm and walked to the door. The family's thanks and see you soon called after him. "You look more than pretty," he said, and brushed a kiss to her forehead. "When the kids leave, activate the alarm." Emily laughed out loud at the command.

The door closed behind him and she proceeded to the dining room. Her children were waiting.

After the flurry of activity that followed the evening meal, the kids were packed and ready to return to their respective homes.

Emily hung on by a slim thread, the accident loop played in her brain, a smile showed on her face. She refused to let the family see what was on her mind as she watched them load the cars. Hang tight Emily, let them go. Play it close to your vest. They won't leave if you open up. And you want them to leave, don't you? Don't you? She didn't know, but she had to.

Hugs and kisses were exchanged on the front steps. Emily observed herself from a distance as if she watched a movie. The Emily she saw looked like an average mother saying goodbye to her children. She saw and heard car doors slam shut. Motors revved, disturbing the silence of the cold night. Headlights cut through darkness, and moved away from the forlorn figure caving in as the big oak doors closed, bringing Emily into real time.

Now the doors were locked. Alarm set. Click. The sound reverberated in the quiet house. Emily listened for echoes of children, of the gathering, of Pat. There were none. Only the tap of her heels. Tap, tap down the hall. Tap, tap, tap as she hurried to her bedroom. No noise on the carpeted floor. She slammed the door, leaned against it breathing hard as if she just finished a race. Clothes stripped off, dropped to the floor. Emily's body trembled. Shaking hands opened drawers searched for warm sweats. Clothes to snuggle in. Groping fingers found them, put them on. Pat's robe. Where is it? Closet, yes. There it is. Wrapped up in it. That's better. Breathing slowed and Emily looked around at the mess she created. Not quite yourself, are you?

Her heart raced, her breath came ragged. What's happening to me? She screamed inside herself, frightened of the unknown. She sat in the stillness of the master bedroom on the bed of memories and the well that ran dry had somehow refilled and she cried and cried and cried.

Emily's eyes flew open. The illuminated clock dial displayed three a.m. The bedside lamp was still on. Slumped against the headboard, her neck felt stiff from the awkward position. She sat up and rotated her head to relieve the cramp in her neck. The phone was next to her, receiver off the cradle. The buzzing noise must have disturbed her slumber.

"I slept six hours. How marvelous. The first real sleep since Pat died." Emily talked to the empty room."Pat died," she repeated. "Maybe if I say that out loud I'll get used to it." Emily closed her eyes but her mind was wide awake. The widow's syndrome. It happened to every widow she knew. They all complained of waking at two or three in the morning, getting up and having a snack, then cleaning closets or doing some other homely task. Her friend Lisa told her to call at any hour because Lisa never slept through the night after her husband died. Emily fought this behavior when she lost Larry and won the battle. She wouldn't succumb this time either. She did have six hours sleep, she rationalized. She could get up, shower, have a snack and maybe send an Email—to whom? That's okay. No one to see what she was doing. No one to get up for, no one to snuggle up to. No one.

Stop it, don't feel sorry for yourself. All right, she replied. Oh boy. Now she was taking both sides of a conversation. Lucky no one was here to catch this. Uh huh. You're a lucky woman, Emily. Yes you are.

With an effort, she pushed the quilt back as if it were filled with nails instead of feathers. She threaded her way through the jumble of last night's clothes and went to the tidy bathroom, a welcome look compared to the chaos of the bedroom. She turned the shower to hot and peeled layers of velour robe and sweats off her thin frame. An unwanted glimpse of herself in the full length mirror convinced her that a nourishing snack was in order.

The shower refreshed her spirit and Emily felt energized as she padded down the hall in sock-clad feet to the kitchen. A peek in the fridge didn't stimulate the appetite gone on strike for two days, but she forced herself to toast a slice of bread, cut up an apple, and microwave a cup of raspberry decaf tea. When the chips were down, that was always a safe bet.

Slowly, she chewed as her mind jumped from one idea to the next. Hold it, girl. You're like a runaway train, out of control. She reached for a pad of paper headed Things-to-Do in numerical order. That's better. Organize yourself. Number one: Change the message on the answer machine, a good start, and pressed the control button to hear the electronic voice tell her what to do. "Press the greeting button to record your message." Emily cleared her throat and did as the machine told her. "Hi kids and anyone else calling. I won't be accepting calls for a day or two because I need to get my brains unscrambled. Don't worry please."

She replayed the message once and twice, listening to the sound of her voice. Sad. Very sad voice. Very sad message. Tears fell, as she took little bites of toast, and splashed on the thin coat of peanut butter. She drew a line through things-to-do Number One and pondered over the next task. She lifted the teacup to her mouth but her hand trembled, spilling the hot red liquid on her list. Emily stared at the paper. The blue ink turned red and ran all over the page. Emily screamed and hurled the pad across the kitchen sending her plate and knife with it. The sound of breaking china and clinking silver stopped her scream.

Emily leapt away from the table, her chair flew backward as she stalked out of the room, hit the light switch and the room was dark. She ran to the exercise room. Her socks skidded on the polished wood floors and up the stairs, but she didn't lose her footing.

The door opened to the stark room whose only adornment was the painting, Emerging Woman. She stood before it breathing hard. Her eyes bore into the eyes of the painted woman.

"Are you challenging me?" she asked the picture. "What do you want?"

The room was silent except for Emily's ragged breathing. She regained control of herself and slipped Pat's robe off; it lay in a heap. She dressed in the white Ge, carefully wrapped her orange belt in place and began the Kata, a series of controlled movements. After an hour, feeling calmer, Emily put the robe on, went back to her bed and fell asleep. The illuminated clock dial showed six o'clock.

The phone rang, breaking the silence of the house, it's strident sound bounced off the walls. The machine picked up a message. Emily slept on, her body curled tight like a fetus in the womb.

A sliver of sunlight marked a line on the bed and moved as the hours ticked by, then disappeared as the sun moved to the other side of the house. The lump that was Emily didn't move.

Door chimes pealed and fists pounded on the front door to no avail. A note slid under the door set the super-sensitive motion detector in action. A high pitched siren went off. Emily stirred, stumbled out of bed and staggered down the hall to disengage the system. The phone rang. It was the surveillance company checking for the password.

Emily picked up, mumbled the password "Pat" and hung up.

Mark's voice called to her. "Emily, please open the door.

Meg's frantic. She called my office. We'll honor your need for privacy, but open the door. I have to tell her I saw you and you're all right."

Emily slid the bolt and unlatched the double-doors. It was dark outside. A cold wind sent a chill through her body.

"Let me in, Em." said Mark.

The door opened wider. Mark stepped in, and shut the door.

"Okay if I turn on a light?"

The house was shrouded in darkness. Emily shuffled down the hall without a word. Mark followed in her wake, talking softly so she wouldn't be frightened.

"I'm right behind you. Meg needs me to call her as soon as possible. Remember when she was little how she had to know where everyone was all the time?" He didn't wait for a reply. "Now that she's pregnant, she needs that assurance again and you know how much she loves you. We all love you. When Laurie got sick and died, you were my rock. Let me be that for you."

She left the hallway, went into the bedroom and fell asleep.

The bedside phone had speed-dial numbers listed. Meg's was at the top. Mark pressed that button. Emily was aware, in the twilight recesses of her mind, of Mark's presence next to her. She felt like a sedated patient in a hospital room fighting her way to consciousness while the seduction of sleep prevented her. She tried to make sense of what he was saying.

"It's Uncle Mark, honey. I'm with your Mom. She's sleeping and I'm going to stay for a while. Maybe overnight. We haven't talked as yet."

Emily's mind said, Don't worry, baby. I'm all right. But she knew she was miles from all right.

"She'll be all right, Meg. I think she's in a state of shock. We know about that, don't we?"

Emily strained to hear Meg's voice. She couldn't.

"Meg, I'll call tomorrow morning before you leave for school. Get some rest. Goodbye."

Don't leave me, Emily's thoughts cried. She felt his kiss on her cheek. That's nice, she thought as she burrowed into sleep.

A nightmare startled her awake. She heard shrieking, her voice yelled, "No, no, no, no, stop."

Emily felt Mark's arms around her. He smoothed her hair

146

and murmured, "You're safe. I'm here."

She pulled away and looked at him. "How did you get in?"

"You opened the door."

"How —"

"Asked and answered. You had a nightmare." She wiped tears away with the edge of a sheet.

"Was it about the accident?"

She nodded.

"Tell me about it. What frightened you the most?"

"Eyes."

"The man you saw?"

"He wants to devour me. Something else. At the funeral, someone shook my hand. He said he was from Pat's office. His name—I'll think of it. Uh, Jerry, Jerry Field. Mark, it didn't sound right and his hand didn't feel good. And one more thing. He didn't take his sunglasses off."

Mark said, "I'll talk to O'Keefe. Let him check it out. Now the question is when did you have something to eat?" he said.

She shook her head. "I don't know."

"Let's go in the kitchen. I'll warm some chicken soup."

That brought a tiny smile to Emily's face. It was an old wife's tale, chicken soup healed all wounds. Maybe it would help. Couldn't hurt.

"Okay. I'm a wreck. I'll wash up and dip my entire body in moisturizer. Be right there."

When she was presentable, they sat close together while Emily finished a steaming bowl of soup.

"If it's all right with you, I'd like to stay overnight. To help you over this time." Emily started to protest but Mark continued. "You are the strongest woman I've ever met. I admire that. Me being here isn't a sign of weakness in you."

His strong hand covered hers. She could smell his after shave lotion, a lime scent, so different from Pat's.

"What day is it?" said Emily.

"Monday, almost Tuesday." Mark looked at his watch. It was after ten. "I'll sleep in the guest room and leave in the morning. I'm due in class for a lecture tomorrow." He kissed the top of her head and left.

Emily sat at the table for a long time. She lost Monday, slept right through, didn't miss much. She counted the leftover noodles in the bowl and stirred them around with her finger, making shapes the way a little kid might do. Or a tormented adult.

After a while, she walked out of the kitchen and down the hall leaving the bowl on the table. That's not like you, Emily. Her mind was in overdrive. At least put it in the sink, run some water so the noodles won't stick to the sides. She didn't listen to the rational Emily. Another Emily took possession of her common sense and she marched to that tune.

At the guest room door, she paused, then tip-toed in to look at Mark. Wonderful. She leaned over and brushed his hair with a kiss. She hurried down the hall toward the back of the house and ran up the stairs to her special room.

Tai Kwan Do was similar to a dancer watching a spot on the wall and turning, she told herself. Chin to right shoulder, chin to left shoulder to prevent dizziness. This is what Tom did when he used to dance. You can do it. Perspiration dripped and blurred her vision. She didn't stop. This would help with kicks and fighting off attackers. Hands on hips, she faced the mirror. Now what? Work out, idiot. Keep yourself firm and quick. The stationary bike gave her a leg workout for twenty minutes. I hate this, she thought, as she rode to nowhere fast. Next came barbells. She looked at the clock. Two in the morning. Time flies when you're having fun. Hit the shower and get some sleep. As she left the room, she stopped before her painting.

"How was that? Am I Emerging?"

Emily dragged her tired body down the dark hall and stopped in mid-stride. Satisfied at her accomplishments, Emily turned lights out. She stumbled into bed. Forgotten was the shower and the vow to clean up her sloppy room. Sleep beckoned. She embraced it as if it were a long lost lover.

Emily slept as in a drug-induced state. Random thoughts crept in to coax her back to the real world, but she resisted. Twisting around on the big bed, she fought to escape back into sleep, but it was over.

"Tuesday. Today is Tuesday. Pat is coming home," she whispered. She cried and held herself tight.

She reached for the phone and dialed Griffith's Funeral

Home, hoping for a machine to pick up. She didn't want to speak to a human person. A voice answered.

"Andrew Griffith speaking." said the voice.

"Mr. Griffith, this is Emily Corwin. Are you delivering the urn today?"

"My driver was out there this afternoon but no one responded to the bell. Are you home now? I can send him again if you'd like."

"Please have the driver come by and ask him to leave it at the door. I'll tape a note outside giving permission so he won't be responsible. Thanks for your courtesy." She hung up before he could say another word.

Emily moved from the bed to the floor in one easy stride. That's better. More energy and she was hungry. Another good sign. Lights on and she blinked at the brightness and the chaos. She caught a whiff of her body as she peeled off smelly sweat pants and a sweat shirt.

Stinging, pulsating needles of hot water struck her body like a massage but she welcomed the alive feeling it brought. She lathered shampoo through her hair. Erotic scenes from past showers with Pat invaded her mind. She pressed hard against her forehead and fought the memories.

"Don't go there," she screamed. "Time for that later. You have work to do, Emily."

She rushed through the shower, towel-dried her hair, dressed in fresh sweats and left the bathroom. Her face was pale and drawn. In a frenzy of activity, Emily brought order to her room. A sound at the front door caught her attention. A car in the driveway stopped then drove away. A sad smile as a few tears trickled down her face. It must be Pat. She looked through the peep hole. No one around. With a furtive motion, she opened the door just wide enough for an arm to reach for the expected package. There it was, waiting for her. She pulled it in, locked the door and slid to the floor, cradling it in her arms. Her heart tightened with pain and grief.

"God, are you there? Anywhere? This is all I have left of my husband. A can of ashes. Why? I don't understand."

She rocked back and forth in the darkness, dozed for a while, then snapped awake, her body stiff and cold from sitting in a cramped position on the flagstone floor, arms still clutched the package that was Pat.

    The little voice spoke: Emily, do something.

    "What?" she said to no one.

    Stand up. Have some soup. Take care of yourself.

    "I can't. I don't want to."

    Make a list. That always helps. And Pat needs attention.

    "Show yourself. I want to hurt you. I need to hurt you."

    Emily listened for the voice but it was gone. She knew the voice was her fragmented self. She forced herself to breathe normally like a real person. This is what I've become, she thought. A woman in pieces. A fine example for my children. Grab hold of your life, your sanity before it's too late.

    She rose and turned on a light, the package held against her chest as if it were a priceless fragile work of art. Emily carried it from room to room, lighting the way through her home. She walked out to the garage, up and down the stairs, and outside to the gazebo where she sat on the swing, all the while humming old favorite tunes. Emily didn't feel the gentle warm breeze. She felt protective of the burden carried so tenderly.

    A man's voice shattered the stillness but didn't penetrate the little world Emily had built around her. She didn't move.

    "Emily, where are you?"

    Mark came around from the front of the house. The real-life Emily knew he was there but the other Emily was in control. She continued to hum the plaintive tune that swirled in her mind.

    "Hi," he said.

    For a moment she didn't acknowledge him. Then her eyes cleared and a smile of recognition came over her face.

    "Hi. Pat's here." She lifted the package.

    Mark draped his suit jacket around Emily and left her alone. She watched him walk to the house now ablaze with lights; his shoulders drooped as he moved. She wondered why he looked sad but she didn't miss a beat of her private melody.

    Time passed and then, like a CD ending, the humming ceased. Emily sprang into action. She moved with a purpose not felt for days. Where did this jacket come from, she wondered as she felt the softness of the wool. Then she recalled Mark's presence.

    Into the storage room she strode, and went right to a large

box marked fragile. Her package placed out of harm's way, she ripped off the tape and extricated an earthenware wide-mouthed jar and lid she'd made a few years before. Emily smiled as she caressed the shape, recalling the thrill of throwing the clay and making it grow. The celadon glaze was beautiful. Three dips in the glaze achieved the look of a horizon. This was perfect. Ashes to ashes, dust to dust — She made a funnel out of rolled cardboard. With caution and loving care, she poured Pat's remains into the jar. As the ashes spilled down, she remembered the lyrics to the tune she'd been humming. It was a lullaby her mother sang to her at bedtime when she was afraid of the dark...Now you have the stars to play with, and the moon to run away with...

Emily went into the tool room. She admired the neat, organized way Pat had stored his tools. All of them so clean. A sledge hammer attracted her attention. Large, heavy and just right for her purpose. Very heavy as she dragged it outside and left it by the door while she ran in to retrieve the empty can. She carried it and with an effort, pulled the hammer along the ground and went into the woods behind the house. Taking aim, she smashed the hammer at the can over and over until it was pulverized, unrecognizable, and her arms couldn't move. Then she slumped against a tree and cried, head in hands, until the well inside her dried. Drained of emotion, Emily stood up surveying the wreckage she'd created.

"Way to go, Emily," she whispered. On leaden legs, she trudged through the cool dark woods, lights from the house to guide her. Time to open Pat's journal.

Surrounded by pillows, a scrubbed clean Emily wrapped in Pat's robe sat in the middle of the bed, the journal in her lap. You delayed as long as possible. Open it. The key seemed to be stuck or was her hand so reluctant to make the final twist? A click and it opened. Sorry, Pat. She turned to one of the last entries, the handwriting not as precise as earlier pages. Written in a hurry or was he excited?

Samuel called with an extraordinary request. Obviously he's desperate or this conversation never would have taken place. I have 24 hours to answer. How can I let him down after all he has done for me? Somehow, that's a laugh, Samuel knows everything, and he found out that I have contacts in industrial espionage through my Army connections. I never used these contacts, I only know about them. He asked me to copy, I'm getting chills as I write, to copy the design for a long range missile with a few modifications. In retrospect, it almost makes me feel like a kid again playing bad guys/good guys back in Minneapolis when I was a kid. A dangerous game but from a distance.

There is money on the table, big stakes. I can renovate the whole house for Emily, pay off her mortgage with cash, make life easier for us.

Rereading this entry, I know my mind is made up. He asked. I'll do it. He said it's urgent, will save lives.

Emily checked the entry date again. Dear God. What a secret and she never guessed. He did that for her. Did he ever really know her or did he conjure up an image of the way he thought she should be? All the questions had no meaning anymore.

There was one last entry. May as well read it. A glass of Chardonnay was necessary for this one, should've had one at the ready with the other page.

Leaving the nest of pillows and blankets, Emily scrambled out of bed and hurried to the kitchen. An opened bottle leftover from the wake stood solitary at the back of the refrigerator, the cork ready to be pulled out. She fumbled with it, poured a full glass spilling a little in haste, wondered if some peanuts would go with it and decided that was silly. Back to the bed and the diary. She stopped to take a sip every few steps, no need to spill wine all over the carpet.

I had a change of heart. Asked him to leave me out of it. He called requesting, then insisting, then begging another favor. A favor. After he promised to leave me out of it. I gave in but no more. God, no more. Lucky last time no one was hurt. Only weapons. Money transferred. Nervous can't sleep stay home Emily concerned oh Emily. She would hate me.

Too terrible, a refugee camp, everyone killed, accident, Samuel takes full responsibility. No. My fault for giving the modified design. Me, the big expert. Me, the mass murderer. What can I do...?

Samuel. My friend, like a father. God will forgive me, Emily never. She must not find out. Let it haunt me. I can live with the memory and keep her safe from harm. My beautiful Emily.

She drained the last of the wine, set the glass on the floor, and searched the air for answers. There were none. The journal cleared up the mystery but she did not understand the man she had married and now he was dead so it was over. No need to ponder, to pick at the remains until they bled. Turn the page. Start a new chapter in your life. And get some sleep. We're all tired.

Emily slept without moving. Two factions of her subconscious waged a battle.

The real Emily: She's like a newborn with days and nights mixed up. She sleeps most of the day and at night, runs herself ragged in the upstairs room. What the hell's going on?

The other Emily: I'm showing her how to cope, that's what I'm doing. This is her life and I'll do what I want with her when I want. It's none of your business.

She's been my business since birth. You'll make her sick.

If she gets sick, we'll be sick. I don't want that to happen but I have to keep her secrets hidden. I warn you, don't interfere. She's been little Miss Perfect too long.

Who are you to say? I've been in control since her beginning.

And where did it get her? Daddy's good girl, Larry's good wife, apple pie mother of the century. Big deal. Once an educated talented, undeveloped person. She didn't let me in until she met Pat.

What are you saying?

Remember, she was just a running coach until she met Pat and now she can fight off an attacker. That was me freeing her from inhibitions.

I was embarrassed.

He loved it but more important, she did. That was a good start.

Anything else you want to boast about?

I take full credit with romance possibilities. Mark Wagner, case in point, although Missy is a quick study.

Maybe we can merge when the crisis is over.

Maybe.

Emily woke up with a fierce headache. She wondered why she was exhausted. Head pounding, she stumbled to the shower full of apprehension. Two aspirins, coffee, and a piece of toast kind-of-day coming up.

One week ago, Pat was killed, thought Emily as she finished breakfast. The college gave me time off and I don't know if I can put myself together to return. Try harder.

She made her way upstairs, compelled to gaze at the painting once more. Lights on, Emily stared at her painting. She pointed at the third shadowy male. "Who are you?"

The other Emily whispered: It will all be revealed. Not to worry. Now get your ass downstairs and have a real meal, for God's sake. You look like shit.

"Thanks," said Emily. "I needed that. And you do have a way with words." This was great. Again she was having a dialogue with herself taking both parts. The mirror reflected a bedraggled, worn woman in need of a hot meal. A bunch of hot meals.

You're an ungrateful bitch, her other voice said. Friends and family love you. Of course they're concerned. You'd be if it was any one of them.

She's right, said the old Emily. The least you can do is return the calls. Assure them you'll take better care of yourself and give a target date for your re-entry into the world.

They'll send for the men in white coats who'll cart you off to never-never land if you don't make contact.

This was swell. Her fragmented selves joined forces. What a team. Better do as they say. It made sense.

She showered, washed her hair, and added a bit of makeup to pale skin. The mirror reflected a bedraggled, worn, clean woman. Not much of an improvement, but today was the day she worked on herself. She hurried to the kitchen, optimistic that she'd find something to eat.

She pressed playback on the answer machine. As disembodied voices floated in the room, Emily stood before the open refrigerator in a quest for sustenance. No Good Samaritan had come in the night to fill the empty box with ready-to-eat nourishment. She reached for an almost full bottle of apple juice bottle of apple juice and drained it down. Not nearly enough. A drop in the bucket.

Meg's voice startled her. "Mother, I called Uncle Mark. He's coming over with groceries. If you don't wake up, I'm going to call the police and you'll have to open the door so they can report to me that you aren't lying in a heap covered in blood or whatever. Goodbye, Mom, I'm late for school. Love you."

Emily shook her head and smiled. "I give up," she called to the machine. "I will eat but I still need time alone no matter what anyone says."

Door chimes rang out. There's Mark right on cue, she thought as she went to answer the insistent knocking. A quick peek through the Seeing Eye and there he was. She disengaged the alarm and opened the door. It was early morning, six forty five. Night lingered before it reluctantly gave way to daylight. A brisk wind blew. Today was a great day to begin living again.

Mark wore a navy worsted suit, jacket open, a red and blue tie blown over one shoulder by the breeze. His arms were laden with grocery bags. His brown hair was disheveled, and a worried look brought frown lines to his handsome face.

Emily stood on tiptoes and brushed her lips to his.

"Thanks for coming," she said. She inhaled his masculine spicy scent, a smile on her face. Seeing him gave her more pleasure than she was ready to admit. "Enter, dear professor."

He set the bags down and pulled her into his arms, a full body hug as if he couldn't get enough of her. She felt him grow hard in response to their tight embrace, heat emanated from his center. A rush chased itself up and down her spine. A tiny flame ignited deep in her body like the first click of a gas burner.

Whoa, Emily. Not so fast, shouted her other voice. Too soon, said the real Emily. For the first time, her fragmented selves agreed on something. The flame clicked to the off position.

"Emily," his words almost lost in her hair, "I've missed you so much. Meg and her command call this morning gave me the excuse to come to the rescue."

Emily bristled at his words. She pulled away.

"Not that you needed rescuing. I know that. But I had to do as she said." His voice deepened. "Her wrath is to be feared."

They both laughed and she knew he pictured the feisty Meg as an adorable blond Toddler, tiny pink pompoms holding twin pony tails one over each ear, standing up for herself amidst her brother and male cousins. Emily moved back into his embrace and reveled in their shared history. The aroma of cooked bacon came from one of the bags and distracted her. Emily sniffed the air.

"Mark, are you my very own caterer?"

"I don't have much time but I thought we could have

breakfast before my lecture this morning. You need to eat more."

Emily said the last few words with him and he looked surprised.

"Everyone left the exact same message so it must be true."

They gathered the groceries and went to the kitchen.

"Let's eat right now. I'm famished," she said. "That's the first time I've used that word in a while."

When Mark wasn't looking, she observed him. He was terrific. A flush colored her face.

He glanced up in mid-bite and caught her watching him.

"What?"

"What do you mean?" Her blush deepened.

"I'll take an educated guess, all right? My antennae is up and it tells me you're thinking of an incredible time in the cabin years ago when no one was around."

He waited for her to confirm or deny. She said nothing but her silence spoke volumes.

"What do I get if I'm right?" he said as he took another bite of eggs.

Thoughtful silence from Emily. They finished breakfast. Mark pushed away from the table. "I heard from John. O'Keefe. Number one. There is no employee or anyone named Jerry Field at Patrick's law firm. Never has been." He held up his hand to continue. "A dune buggy paint job was reported from a body shop in Macon, Georgia. Those vehicles are rare. Blue chips matched the ones recovered at the beach. The owner of the vehicle paid in cash. He stayed nearby for two days waiting for the dune buggy."

Mind spinning, Emily said, "Did he get the license number?"

"Stolen plates. Clever man."

"Description?"

"Good girl. Yes, an artist interviewed the mechanic and made a drawing." Mark removed a sketch from his briefcase and placed it on the table.

Not a perfect likeness but him. "It's the man on the beach. The glasses, the shape of his face, and the eyes. We've got him, right?" She jumped up and began to pace.

Mark stopped her. "Not so fast. There's a lot of solid work

ahead for the department but at least they're on the right track. The new dune buggy color is red. Popular color for the younger crowd. He'll stand out as an older man. You said he was mature."

She nodded. "About fiftyish give or take, wide shoulders, gray hair, thinning. Wait a minute. That's a description of the man at the funeral. The unknown Jerry Field."

Mark polished his glasses. "Bold move to come to the funeral. Bold and reckless. He pulled Emily close. "He seems to be obsessed with you, my dear. He made it a point to touch you. Most killers would observe from a distance." He thought for a moment. "Stay close to home. Call John. Here's his number and I'll call him on my way to the University."

At the door he said, "I hate to leave, Emily, but keep it together, please. I have to run, eager students await. How about dinner later?"

"I don't know."

"When you're ready, let me know and I'll arrange something special."

Emily nodded. She mouthed thanks, too filled with emotion to speak. Mark kissed the top of her head and let himself out.

"Lock up," he called and Emily heard the door shut.

She followed his advice. When she engaged the alarm system, the red light took on a life of its own. She was caught by the power, imaginary or real. It seemed to say, You're safe for now, for now. For a few minutes she had relaxed, enjoyed Mark's company, felt carefree. Then excited with further news about the mystery man, she decided to let Mark talk to John O'Keefe. Good. An improvement.

With care, she unpacked groceries and organized the kitchen. Things were looking up. She hit the playback button again and the messages kept her company as she tidied up.

The voice of Jesse, her best friend: "We suffer without you. Call." Lola, the artist: "Enough of the solitude. I want to hear from you." Emily chuckled. She made a note to call them today, maybe. Definitely call Meg was at the top of the list. She hit speed dial #1, Meg's number. This was a good time to call since Meg was at work.

Another idea came to her and she jotted it down. Email to Erle Lim in California. She wondered how he was.

A compulsion hit Emily like a gale force wind. She stopped,

shook her head but it wouldn't leave. Work out, run; work out, run. Hurry. Time is running out. Hurry. Her breath came fast, then faster and she ran to her private room upstairs. She was home alone with the alarm on but found it necessary to lock the room. Only then did Emily calm down. Peace flooded through her as she went through the routine she'd created two weeks before. It was as if an old friend kept her company with exercise equipment and the painting, Emerging Woman.

Time to start running again, thought Emily. Mark said to stay close to home. The beach was at her doorstep close enough. Dare she try the beach? Maybe it was too soon, just three weeks since Pat— her thoughts trailed off. She plodded to the bathroom to check out her tousled self. Not so bad. Eating a bit more, sleeping better, soon you'll look like the old Emily. You'll never be the same and that's okay. Try going on the beach. Worst that can happen is you'll freak out and go home. No big deal.

Dressed in a tank top and running shorts, she ate a piece of toast with a glass of orange juice, pocketed the cell phone, grabbed a bottle of water and away she went. If she could do this, she was ready to get back to work. The substitute coach was fine but she wasn't experienced. The next step would be to invite the kids for dinner and also get back to the club. She went into the garage. There was her new white Jeep, Pat's surprise gift last month. Blood money? "Thanks Pat," she whispered. His Mercedes was parked next to it. Dusty, unused, a forlorn look about the gray convertible. Emily wrote his name in the dust. Closing the door, She ran to the back and headed north on the beach. She hadn't left the house or driven the car in three weeks. The longest and shortest three weeks of her life. How had she filled all those solitary days and nights? Time had no beginning or end for her. Well, she was on the way back to normality now. Emily pulled her hair through a scrunchy. She glanced in the mirror and noticed gray hair at the roots needed a touch-up. Never did keep that appointment at the beauty shop. She wondered if anyone had canceled it. Stop, stop. Put everything out of your mind and run. This is a test. See if you can pass.

The day was bright and warm. April in all its glory with the promise of hope and rebirth, Emily's favorite time of year.

She ran, not stopping for a drink of water, not stopping to catch her breath, she ran away from herself trying to get back to herself.

A male voice from behind startled her. She flinched but kept running. "On your left," a deep voice said and a man passed her. No one ever passed her. She was too fast. Emily couldn't stop. Her feet flew, took wing, in the zone as she was that final day. She ran as far as she did that fateful morning and stopped. Looked around. Had the feeling of being watched. The truth was, someone did watch and she better use caution. Shivers. Time to head back. Back to her life, back to reality. She turned, paused to take a long pull of water, and plodded back, placing one foot in front of the other, regrouping with each step.

You did it, you really did it. All the way home, that was her mantra. Pink blossoms on the hydrangeas cascaded to the ground. Emily stooped to examine the flowers and smiled. Nestled up against the house were bunches of grape hyacinths. Somehow they survived among cactus and other succulents. High dunes protected the back of the house from the ocean breeze but today it was too hot, sun too strong in the clearing to her home.

"Pat, you made me crazy with your caveman mentality. Me Tarzan, you Jane." She laughed in spite of herself and unlocked the slider. She hurried to disengage the alarm, closed the door, and reset it. The red light blinked a warning. Do not touch, it said. She hated this routine, resented all the precautions Pat was devoted to. She was home safe and as sound as she could manage right then. In fact, doing pretty good for three weeks.

In the house, Emily's first impulse was to cocoon, but she fought against it. Her fragmented selves jumped in. She held her head as they warred.

Too easy to get back in the established pattern, said the other Emily. Don't do it.

The old Emily jumped in. You're tired, dear. It's okay to stay home and rest. The feisty one hurled insults. Oh shut up. You're enabling her to cop-out. The selves overlapped. When did you become her psychologist? She has to grow up. Cooperate or you're history. There's room for both of us, y'know.

Emily stripped off damp clothes, dropped them in the hamper and stepped into the shower. Hot water eased aches from the pounding she took during the run. A massage would feel great right about now, she thought as she dried off and dressed in a warm-up suit.

Breakfast and phone calls were next on the agenda. With a

phone tucked against her ear and shoulder, she poured a cup of milk and oatmeal in a saucepan over a low flame and stirred. No answer at the beauty salon. She checked the time. It was 8:30. Too early. Next, she hit speed-dial for Meg and left a message."Hi honey, I'm feeling better and hope all of you can come for dinner Saturday. Hope you're available. Call me. I'm ready for a visit."

She felt good, almost like a regular person. A sprinkle of brown sugar over the steaming oatmeal and Emily was ready to eat a stick-to-your-ribs breakfast. She smiled, remembering her Mom who had labored over the range, no instant cereal so many years ago.

She called Tom and spoke to his machine, then got the same result with Amanda's phone. Maybe they'd all come Saturday. She missed her children.

Ashley answered at the hairdresser's. Dale could take her at ten thirty for color, cut, and a manicure. "And guess what," Ashley said, not waiting for an answer, "Jackie's getting married!"

"Wonderful," Emily said. "Are you available for a massage today?" said Emily.

"Come at 10 o'clock. I can give the massage first and we'll work you in for the rest."

Emily thanked her and hung up. An overhaul is what she really needed. She packed a change of clothes and started for the door. Mark said to stay at home. Well, she wasn't going far from home. Just to little old St. Augustine.

Emily hung up, grabbed her keys and headed for the magic of her hairdresser, ready to be pampered. As she maneuvered through the narrow streets, she thought about Mark. He'd been at her side whenever she let him and even when she was distant, he assured her that it was okay. He'd seen her at her worst and yet he kept coming back. Oh God, he must have seen all that gray hair growing in. Her cover was blown. Now he knew she wasn't a natural ash brown and sun streaks weren't always from the sun. Big deal. So what if she had no secrets.

She spotted a parking place and pulled in. Sport bag with a change of clothes in hand, Emily groped for the cell phone. A quick call to him. Maybe she could meet him for lunch.

His secretary, Lenore Hammond answered. She'd been his right hand forever. "Professor Mark Wagner, good morning."

"I sent a card, Emily. Professor said not to call. You have

my best thoughts, my dear."

"Today's the first time I've gone out. The hairdresser's waiting for me. I need all of her talent today. Thanks for your kind wishes. He can reach me on the cell phone around one o'clock, if he has a minute."

"He'll make time with you, don't worry." An awkward pause. "Sorry, a Freudian slip." Humor in her voice. "I meant, he'll make time for you, of course. Goodbye." She was gone.

A break in the flow of cars and Emily ran across the street, threw open the door and inhaled the perfumed scent of the salon, glad to be alive.

Dale's stiletto heels clicked on the tile floor, amazing spiky long hair flew in every direction, as she hurried to greet Emily. What a woman. Her black Lycra pants looked as if they were painted on her slim shape, with enough cleavage to cause an accident on the oldest street in America; she enfolded Emily in a hug.

"Help. I'm being smothered by the boobs that ate Cleveland," said Emily, laughing. It was their special greeting repeated over and over for at least fifteen years.

Dale held her at arm's length, and assessed the ravages of the past few weeks. "You look like shit."

"Thanks. Fix it."

"Ashley's waiting for you in the massage room. Get your ass in there and we'll get to work."

An hour later, Emily rolled off the table and stood on rubbery legs. Her bones felt soft, tension gone from her neck and shoulders. Time for hair transformation. Dale applied mysterious potions to Emily's head as Tina labored over neglected hands.

"I'm giving you highlights. They've faded." Dale said.

"Whatever. I'm at your mercy," Emily said, in a sleepy voice.

Three hours passed. In the dressing room, Emily slipped a yellow v-neck silk sweater over her head, careful not to muss Dale's masterpiece hair-do. Highlights that looked like sun streaks were artfully scattered through Emily's hair. A shine spray added luster. She pulled on tapered, stone-washed light blue jeans. After three weeks of wearing baggy shorts and pajamas, the jeans felt fine. She surveyed herself in the mirror. Here I am, she thought, looking better than expected. She approved of the transformation.

Emily was relaxed, her hairdresser was exhausted.

"Emily, I know you've had a terrible tragedy in your life. You had one not so long ago, but I've never been so challenged with you in all the years I've worked on that great head of hair. What the hell have you done to yourself?" Dale said.

She continued to admire her reflection and smiled ruefully at the question.

"I don't know what to say, except thanks. It's been a rough time and it's not over but all your skill came through for me today. I feel reborn or at least able to go forward today."

The women hugged, Emily paid the bill and left. She dialed Mark one more time. If he wasn't in, she'd head home.

"Lenore, did he return?"

"Came in two minutes ago. Hold please."

Emily crossed the street, aware of an admiring glance from a passing motorist. Mark's voice came on the line.

"Emily, where are you?"

She slid the gym bag into her car. "St. George Street in town. If you're free for lunch, I'd love to see you. My treat."

"Meet me in the kitchen." He hung up.

She stared at the phone, then hit the end button and laughed. That was so funny coming from Mark. More like the Mark from olden days when the two couples were carefree, enjoying good times with each other. Now she and Mark were all that was left from the golden days of friendship. He meant to meet her at the Mandarin Garden. She put more money in the meter and walked over.

There he stood, looking mystified at the outside menu and the artistic displays. So many goodies, so little time is what his posture seemed to say. He is one great looking man, she thought. Needs a hair trim maybe although she really liked the way his dark hair curled, just a little bit, over the shirt collar.

"Hi, Handsome."

Emily's voice startled him. He looked up from his reverie, a slow grin, and then he reached for her hand.

"I've missed you, Emily, the real Emily." He looked her up and down, turning her in a full circle to get the effect. "You're better, aren't you?" She nodded. "And you look beautiful but why are you away from home? I asked you to stay close."

"I just came from an overhaul at the salon. Massage and the works. Needed a Dale fix. Let's go in."

After ordering, they had a chance to talk without shadows of home, Pat, and death to interrupt.

"I'm all mixed up, Mark. My emotions seesaw all the time. I'm sad, then intense, then briefly I feel a sense of well being and then I'm frightened of allowing myself to feel good."

"Sounds normal to me. It will take time but I'm here to help you over the rough spots."

She breathed deeply, knowing his words were true. "I'll be patient with myself. I promise."

Over a shared plate of chicken and broccoli, Emily confessed some of the fears she had. "I hate the alarm routine at the house. It upsets me having to use it every time I leave and return. I look up at the hidden cameras watching me and I want to scream."

Mark listened as she spilled out her anger and fears. He patted her hand and said, "You might move out, at least for a while, until you decide what to do. Then you won't have to deal with the alarm." He helped himself to more chicken. "Eat, please. You're working yourself up and I'm finishing the food."

She stared at him in amazement. "Why didn't I think of that? It's such a simple solution for the time being. I'm not married to the house. I'm not married —" They looked at each other as the food got cold.

Emily toyed with a piece of chicken and it fell out of the chopsticks. She changed the subject. "Any more word from John O'Keefe?"

Mark laid the chopsticks down. "This dune buggy that struck Pat is an antique, popular about thirty five years ago. That's one of the reasons the owner of the body shop paid close attention. He said it's in perfect shape except for —some damage to the hood. O'Keefe's been checking on records for that kind of vehicle in our area. Whoever owns it keeps it hidden-garaged privately. Maybe in one of the large homes at the beach. You said you feel as if someone is watching you. Could be him hiding right under our noses."

He leaned across the table to wipe an errant crumb from the

corner of her mouth. "I have to run. Come on. I'll walk you back to your car."

Emily paid the bill and followed him outside. "I haven't seen a dune buggy in years but your theory sounds like it fits." She took a deep breath. "Maybe I should move out for a while but I'll be damned if I'm going to run away."

"I'll call you later and we can discuss your worries. Together we can formulate a plan to help you feel safe." Mark smiled at her. "I like that word, together."

She frowned; the worried feeling crept over her. "Mark, where would I move? Do you mean rent an apartment or stay in a hotel?"

He adjusted his glasses and steered her across St.George.

Oh, Oh. What's he up to? she wondered.

"There is a room in my place that's vacant right now, no strings attached and the price is right."

Emily smacked his arm and smacked it again in case he didn't get it and when they arrived at her car, she pecked him on the cheek.

As Emily drove home, she mulled over their conversation. In a very oblique way, that rascal asked her to live with him. Clever, professor. No way was that going to happen, not now if ever. She had to become her own person first. He was delicious though.

At home, she pulled into the garage and entered the house. No smile on her face now, she

The answer machine was on overload. Calls from Meg, Amanda, and Tom confirming Saturday's dinner. Good. Calls from the gang. Good. A call from a stranger, a Jim Martin claiming to be Pat's lawyer, says he called five times to no avail, urgent that he speak to her ASAP. Left office and home phone plus cell phone number. Replay that message.

Write down all the numbers. Last message from another stranger. "Mrs. Corwin, this is Joe Taylor. I don't know if Pat mentioned my name to you." Fat chance, thought Emily. "I'm his insurance representative and I have several checks for you. Rather than mail them, it might be better to hand deliver them to you. Please call this number day or night."

Sounds interesting. Ah Pat, you couldn't bend your rules and take me into your confidence. Maybe if we'd had more time. Well, it's moot now. Emily finished the soup, picked up the phone and returned the first call.

"Jim Martin, please. This is Emily Corwin returning his call."

She smiled when a young boy called to his father, "Daddy, a lady wants to talk to you."

A deep male voice said, "Jim Martin here."

"This is Emily Corwin returning your call."

"I've been worried about you. I was at the funeral and paid my respects, but you probably don't remember me. You were surrounded by family and friends. I didn't want to intrude."

"I don't remember you, Mr. Martin. You called for what reason?"

"I am Pat's lawyer. I drew up his last will."

Emily was silent. She hadn't thought about a will, had no idea where a copy might be and didn't know who the beneficiary was. She never went through his papers and of course, she should have.

"Mrs. Corwin, are you still there?"

"Yes. You want to meet with me and soon. Is that it?"

"Yes. Are you free tomorrow early afternoon?

"I am. Would you mind coming to my home? Today was the first time I drove since Pat was killed."

"I can be there at one o'clock. See you then. Goodbye."

"Wait. Don't you need directions?"

"No. I have your address. 13 Atlantic View. Correct?"

"Yes. Pat's insurance man called me. Maybe he can be here when you come."

"Oh, Joe Taylor. That would be opportune."

"You know him?" she said.

"We go way back. I have to run now. My son is waiting for a bedtime story. Goodbye."

Emily slumped in her chair, all energy drained. Another bitter reminder of how Pat cut her out of decisions that should have been made by both of them. She wondered if he left anything to her. She could live well without his support but in these times, a

165

little help would be appreciated. Jim Martin knew the answers.

She'd have to wait. And what about Joe Taylor and the mystery checks. Sounds like an impenetrable Good Old Boys Club. No ladies invited. Do they have a secret handshake? Deep breaths Kathleen, take deep breaths. Inhale through your nose to the count of eight; hold it for eight; exhale through your mouth for eight. Repeat. Her heart rate slowed and relaxation replaced tension.

Somehow the bright spring day had turned to dusk. She sat on the patio for a while listening to the waves and watching white caps roll in a line and retract, roll and retract. Hibiscus and hydrangeas competed in a beauty contest as pampas grass swayed back and forth. Stubby palm trees planted years before lined the old boards to the sand. Beautiful. Yet somewhere, not too far away, a stranger wanted her enough to kill for her. Why?

Emily turned her back on the beauty, entered the house, locked up and made her lonely way to the bedroom. She fell on the bed, curled up and slept.

What does my beauty think of lying in the lounge chair staring out at the beach? Does she think of me and wonder when we'll meet? Clifford Lansdale dropped his coffee cup in the sand where he lay hidden from view. Soon, my little love, soon. When you least expect me, I'll reach out and you will welcome your new lover. He crabbed away from his hidey hole and scurried home.

"Mark pick up, it's Emily. I know it's too early but you said to call at any hour so here I am."

"Good morning. You caught me in mid-shower. Wish you were here. I'm dripping with soap."

A shiver ran through her, warmth spread to dark places. "I'm sorry but something's come up and I need to discuss it with you."

"Hearing your voice caused something to come up. Hurry over. You can dry my back." An uncertain laugh.

"Mark Wagner, behave yourself and thanks for the offer. I'll take a rain check, if it's all right with you."

"It will have to be all right. What's up?" A pause. They broke up with laughter. "I'll rephrase the question. How can I help?"

"Mark," said Emily, "calm down, rinse off, and call back."

She hung up, poured another cup of coffee, and continued

making notes. Her mind whirled with thoughts of Jim Martin, the lawyer she didn't know existed before last night, and Joe Taylor, the insurance man she never heard of who said he had checks made out to her. This time she'd be smart with any money or property left to her. She wrote BE SMART in capital letters. 'Don't let anyone take advantage. Discuss everything with Mark. He's the only person living who is completely interested in my welfare. The kids are terrific but MONEY CORRUPTS. No matter how sincere Jim Martin is, remember he was Pat's lawyer, not yours. Get a copy of the will in case you can't find Pat's copy, and give Mark all legal papers.'

The phone rang. "I'm dressed. You missed your big chance," said Mark.

"Is the key word big?" said Emily. "Oh God. Now you've got me doing it. I can't believe I said that."

"Neither can I but I like it. We're entitled to have a little fun with words and it's safe. What's on your mind?"

"A lawyer called last night. Jim Martin. Do you know him?"

"Yes. He has a decent reputation. What did he want?"

"He's bringing Pat's will here at one o'clock. And an insurance man, Joe Taylor, called and said he has checks for me."

"I know him. He's a reputable broker. Is he coming today?"

"I'll call him soon. Maybe he can be here around one. What should I do? Talking about finances makes me feel inadequate. Math was and still is my worst subject."

"I'll call when I speak to Ellen. She has my appointment book. One o'clock is usually left open for lunch so that time frame might work. Don't let either of them talk about investments or money and property." Emily sighed with relief.

"You and I will decide how to best protect your assets. You'll hear from me in a couple of hours. 'Bye."

She put a spoonful of sugar in the coffee and took a sip. What the hell was she doing? She didn't use sugar and the coffee was cold. Disgusting. She pressed fingertips to her temple. Her brain was seesawing again. When would she get on an even keel? Way off balance this morning. Lucky she had Mark to help her through this muddle. He inspired confidence. She felt strong with him on her side.

You're lucky? said the old Emily. Two husbands dead in

less than two years. You need a keeper, that's what you need.

Shut up with the negative digs, said the other one. That doesn't help. You're like Iago pouring doubts in her ear. Drip, dripping your poison.

"Stop, stop, please stop," screamed Emily. Emily ran to the sink, splashed cold water on her face, and forced herself to stop. She sunk to the floor, a dish towel covered her face, and cried until the well emptied.

Voices whispered. Come on. Get moving. There's time for a run.

Don't go. It's not safe. Warring voices. Nothing happened yesterday when she ran. Face the demon and survive. She stood. The little crisis was over. Don't look in the mirror. You won't like what you see. Get dressed and run.

Emily dialed Joe Taylor's number and left a message requesting an appointment at her home at one. She grabbed a bottle of water and hurried out. Billowing black clouds threatened rain. She could deal with that kind of threat. She returned home as raindrops pelted the car. April showers. The ones that bring May flowers. She prayed for flowers.

Not so bad, she thought as she showered. Two days of running and still alive. No monster on the beach. Take time to dress, makeup with care. Look your best today. Get back in the habit of taking care of yourself.

At one o'clock sharp, three men were at the door. She scrutinized the line-up through the peephole. Can't tell the players without a program. Alarm disengaged, doors opened, and the gracious hostess smiled her guests inside. Mark had his distinguished professor-look on his face. He shook hands with Emily as if they were polite strangers. She stifled a grin and waited for the newcomers to introduce themselves. Joe Taylor squeezed her hand with a bit too much enthusiasm. She winced. A small man with an abundance of energy, he waved an envelope at Emily. Mark gave him a calm-down look. Joe responded like a pet would to a command from the master. Jim Martin introduced himself and shook hands with Mark, deference obvious. So much for the male sniffing, thought Emily. She knew of Mark's reputation as a distinguished professor of law but this bowing and scraping was beyond her expectations. Delightful. Now what?

Mark steered them into Pat's office to conduct business, the one room in the house Emily had no say in decorating. It reeked of testosterone. Gleaming dark oak floors, walls paneled in dark pine, displayed his collection of framed awards and trophies lined the walls, all stating that Patrick Corwin won first place in countless competitions of many kinds. Professor, lawyer, and insurance agent seemed to be in awe of their surroundings.

Joe and Jim sat on the visitor's chairs; Emily sat at Pat's desk, a place she'd never before inhabited. Mark stood behind her.

"Gentlemen, thank you for coming here. I appreciate your taking the time in your busy day to make a house call."

Jim said, "I have a copy of the will for you. Do you want to read it before I proceed?" The informal gathering had taken on a formal atmosphere.

"Yes," Emily said, opening the will she had never thought about. Didn't know such a document existed. How naïve can you get. You never learn. Her heartbeat quickened in anticipation. Mark leaned over her shoulder, his scent filling her nostril. Better than aromas from a bakery.

"Pat left most everything to you with a generous gift to Amanda," Mark said. He spoke solely to Emily, looking deep in her eyes. His intense gaze said: I love you. She flushed with heat reading his look. His voice said, "His stock portfolio lists you as the sole beneficiary. All insurance policies are in your name. All personal belongings are given to you." Mark looked up at Jim. "I assume you have the papers in order for the transfer."

The words hit her hard. Money received from Samuel when Pat did something unimaginable in order to leave money for her. Dear God. His secret had become her secret.

Jim appeared flustered. He squirmed in his chair, adjusted his tie, and nodded as he handed a leather binder with Pat's name embossed in gold to Emily.

"Thank you," said Emily, and handed the folder to Mark. He laid the papers on the polished surface of the antique desk, sorted them in his meticulous way. Each piece of paper fell under his scrutiny, each detail examined until he finished and pronounced everything accounted for.

Emily followed as best she could, thrilled that he was there for her as he had promised almost a month ago. The room was hushed; the lawyer held his breath until Mark announced all was satisfactory. Mark gathered the papers and placed them to one side of the desk. He turned his attention to Jim Taylor, who cringed under his gaze.

"My turn," said Sam, an embarrassed grin on his narrow face. "I wrote this term policy for Pat when he was forty. He checked the accidental death box on the policy at that time. You are the sole beneficiary and receive double indemnity due to the unfortunate circumstances of his death." He handed an official looking check to her. Emily's eyes widened at the amount. "The company Pat represented valued his services highly as evidenced by the coverage they gave him. Accidental death was covered on this policy as well." He handed her another check. "You have my sympathy for your loss. Pat was a special client and friend. I'll miss him. He was one-of-a-kind. If there's anything I can do for you, please contact me. We can talk about any policy you might want for yourself —" Mark cut him off with a hand gesture.

"Thank you for coming," said Emily.

The meeting was over. The men stood for another round of handshakes and the door closed behind them.

Emily was pensive, mixed feelings surrounded her. In one fell swoop she had become an independently wealthy woman, thanks to Pat's foresight. In the end, he had protected her to the best of his ability. She turned to Mark and caught him watching her, a bemused expression on his face.

"What?" she said.

"What's your feeling about those men?"

"I don't understand your question."

He checked his watch. "I have to leave soon but while the meeting is fresh in your mind, let's be comfortable." He led Emily to the living room where they settled on the couch. "They were bearers of good news. Because Pat was diligent in his responsibility to you, your life is now financially secure. My question is did they leave happy in that knowledge or did they leave disgruntled, unfulfilled?"

Emily pondered over the question. What was he getting at? "They weren't happy to leave empty handed. She looked at him, like a schoolgirl taking a test. "Did I get it right?"

He beamed showing a flash of dimples Emily couldn't resist. She reached over to touch the face she'd cared about for so many years. He caught her hand in his and kissed each finger.

"I wanted to see if you understood the dynamics of the

meeting." She wasn't listening. His kisses distracted her. "Listen for just a moment. They are decent men but they are business men. They each hoped for reciprocity from you. They brought gold to the party. You took the gold and gave nothing in return." Emily was puzzled. "Jim hoped, maybe even expected you to ask him to draw up a will for you. Perhaps you'd ask him to be your lawyer, give advice to you, to have a working agreement with you. Instead he found me here, which pleased him not at all, I'm certain. And what did you say upon receiving all the papers from Pat's estate?"

"I said thank you. And goodbye."

"Exactly." Mark kissed her fingers again. "And Joe Taylor brought major dollars and placed them in these lovely hands. He wasn't thrilled when he left either."

"I understand. He hoped I'd buy a policy or two. Instead, I thanked him and showed him the door. That wasn't very nice of me, was it?"

"It was perfect. You didn't allow the moment to seduce you into purchasing anything. If you choose to do business with one or both of them, you'll think it over and decide at a less emotional time. And speaking of seduction, I'm having a difficult time thinking of anything but you."

Mark pulled her into his arms, hands stroking hair, inhaling the fragrance unique to her causing his trousers to tighten. He groaned.

"I have to go." He stood up with evidence of his ardor pointing at her. "Will you dine with me tonight?"

Emily gave him a thoughtful look. "Dinner," she said. "Just dinner."

What an interesting afternoon. She never had any real business experience. With Mark's help, she had said all the right things. Am I smart or what, she asked herself. It's the what that concerned her. She was very drawn to Mark. There. She said it. Could she confide in anyone? No. She could only confide in Mark. He would give her good advice.

Emily chuckled, got up, locked the door and went to Pat's study. The checks had to be in a safe place. There was a safe behind a framed award. Pat never told her about it. One more secret. A mystery she'd have to solve. She found it quite by accident while dusting his awards. Now where would Pat keep a record of the combination? Perhaps he never had a written record.

Oh, stop. Just go ahead and look.

She started a methodical search. At first she carefully searched every drawer, every book turned upside down. After thirty minutes, in a frenzy she flung his treasures all over the floor. The room was a disaster, she was a mess, and no combination was uncovered. She panted from exertion and frustration. She sat in the middle of chaos and forced herself to calm down. She thought of dates he might have used for a combination. Birthdays? No, too common for an uncommon man. Anniversaries? No way. Wait a minute. She walked to the wall safe, shook her hands in the air to get the circulation flowing, then placed a hand on either side of the safe and leaned her forehead against the lock. She breathed slowly and concentrated. After a while, she smiled. Her fingers moved the dial twice full circle to clear, then 3 to the right-15 to the left-99 to the right. Bingo. The door swung open. Numbers she'd seen several times in the journal.

It was a small safe. She looked in, expecting diamonds and gold to sparkle. What did a person keep in a safe? There were several envelopes. Disappointed, Emily pulled them out, sat in Pat's chair and opened a large manila envelope marked Emily. With trembling hands, she ripped open a smaller bulky envelope also marked Emily. Inside, nestled in tissue, was a cassette tape. She looked around for the cassette player, and dropped the tape in. Pat's rich baritone voice filled the room all. She held her hands together and prayed. Dear God, please give me strength. Please, please.

"Dearest Emily, You're listening to this so I'm dead. When we met last year, I couldn't believe a wonderful, normal, happy person could fall in love with me. Every day I lived in fear of you leaving me; finding another less damaged man; or just getting tired of me. I didn't tell you because it would make me seem weak and I wanted to be a strong husband. So I hid my fears the way I've done all my life. There isn't much more to say, dearest Emily. Take care of yourself. I've provided for your future with solid assets. I have provided for Amanda as well. I do have one request. Stay close to her, my Emily. If she's ever in need, please take care of her. Maybe you could arrange a college fund for any children she and Meg might have. When her mother died, she received all the jewelry and other personal articles of value. I want you to have everything of mine to disperse or keep as you wish. One last item, Emily dearest, and this is the most difficult."

Pat's voice wavered, then broke. Silence on the tape.

"You are a beautiful, desirable woman. I hope you'll find a good mate. Know that you have my blessing. Your friend Mark is in love with you. You have a history with him. I ran a check on him and he passed with flying colors."

Emily smiled. This was so typical of the thorough Pat.

"He's someone who would be good enough for you. I'm not telling you what to do but he's more than okay. Don't forget me Emily. We'll meet in a better place. I love you forever and beyond."

The tape ended. He never referred to his journal. With all the preparations he'd made in the unlikely event of his demise, there was no provision for his deadly secret.

Emily sat for a long time, her head on Pat's desk, cradled by folded arms. The phone rang. She didn't move to pick it up. It rang and rang. She reached out and lifted the receiver.

"Hello," her voice subdued, cautious.

"Emily, it's Mark. What's wrong?"

"What's right is the question."

"Talk to me," he said.

"I need some time to think. Can we meet for breakfast tomorrow?"

"It would have to be early."

"Like seven?"

"Yes."

"Okay. Pelican Way Diner at seven."

"What about dinner? Do you have anything more than a carrot in the refrigerator?"

"I don't know. Don't worry about me. I'll manage."

"I'll leave something delicious at your door in half an hour. See you in the morning. Bring the checks. We'll discuss options and decide together what's best for you. Good night."

She listened to the dial tone and hung up. Pat was right. Mark was more than okay. Weary but determined to restore the room to order, Emily went to work. When she finished, she left the room, clicked off the light and shut the door. The journal was high on a shelf in the bedroom closet. She stood in front of the fireplace and lit a match to newspaper. Soon the dry firewood caught, a good blaze started, the warmth chasing chill from her body. She tore the journal pages to pieces and tossed them into the flames. They danced into ashes and were gone.

"Pat," she whispered, "Secrets are dust."

Emily heard a car door open and footsteps in the driveway. She smiled. Mark's catering service. Yes, he was more than okay. Dinner as promised, outside the door.

Emily sat cross-legged in the middle of her bed, fresh from the shower, face shiny with night cream, hair brushed back in a ponytail. She tried to organize plans for the Saturday gathering of her small clan but her thoughts were scattered as they'd been since Pat died. She called Mark.

"What are you doing Saturday night?" said Emily.

"I'll be in California on business Friday so I arranged to stay over and catch up with my sons. Haven't seen them for a few months," said Mark. "What did you have in mind, I hope?"

Emily laughed. "Ever the opportunist, you rascal. I invited the kids for dinner. Four weeks have gone by since they were here. I'm ready for their company and hoped you'd join us."

"Thanks for including me in a family gathering. I'll be back Sunday. How about dinner?"

"I accept. Call when you get home. Safe journey and love to the boys."

Emily hung up. Pillow talk for the older set, she thought. Talk about kids and mundane stuff with a warmer current pulsing underneath. That was enough for now. As Mark had said, it was safe talk.

She took a notepad and pen from the nightstand and concentrated on Saturday's menu. Jumbo shrimp cocktail, poached salmon, or maybe a crown pork roast and roasted new potatoes with steamed vegetables. Crème brulee for dessert. Sounds good. Or a standing rib roast, or pot roast, roast turkey, baked ham— she started to cry. Her hands pressed her head in an attempt to stop the scrambled thoughts. She cried harder, her body shook with sobs bordering on hysteria.

The voices called. Emily, it's okay. They spoke together in harmony, gentle this time. Be patient. You're coming out of a depression. It's okay to feel the seesawing again. Time to sleep. Good times are coming. The kids will surround you with love and you'll feel better. Sleep now.

Emily pulled the comforter up to her neck and curled into a ball. Her last thought before drifting off: I'll feel better.

Chimes rang, phones rang. A pounding at the door got her attention.

"Coming, I'm coming," said Emily, as she stumbled out of bed and dragged her body to the door. She looked through the peephole. Tom and Julie waggled fingers at her. She threw open the door. "You're not supposed to be here 'til tomorrow."

They exchanged a quick glance before entering the house. Tom ran to the alarm and turned it off.

"Mom, you said Saturday and today's Saturday." He dropped his bag and picked her up as he always did in greeting. "Are you sick?"

"No honey. Why do you ask?"

"You're wearing pajamas and it's two in the afternoon."

"How can it be Saturday? When I went to bed it was Thursday."

Julie gathered their belongings and headed for the kitchen. "Come on. I'll make coffee or whatever Mom wants."

Emily looked at herself in the entrance hall mirror. "I'm wearing pajamas. I can't believe it. I slept right through Friday like I was Mom Van Winkle. The last thing I remember is trying to plan a menu for Saturday. Today." She turned to look at Tom. "Do you think something's wrong with me? Why would I sleep so long?"

Tom yelled, "Julie, come back. We need your opinion."

"What's the matter?"

"Mom wonders why she slept through Friday. Do you think she's ill?"

Julie put her arms around Emily. "How do you feel, Mom?"

"I feel healthy. Rested and famished. What a marvelous feeling," said Emily. "Kids, I think I've been in a state of shock and I'm just crawling out of it."

"That sounds right on target to me," said Julie. "You just diagnosed yourself. I bet you haven't slept well this month."

"No. I hardly slept at all. Well, I'm caught up now." Emily

smiled. "I'll shower and you two make something wonderful to eat. Mama is hungry." Emily ran down the hall to her bedroom.

Tom and Julie squeezed hands. "I think she's right in her assessment," said Julie. "I'm treating a woman who has post-traumatic stress disorder. She returned from duty in Iraq and saw sights she couldn't deal with. Now that I see Mom, she fits the pattern."

"I thought Mom needed privacy when she told us to stay away. Maybe she should have been under a doctor's care. Maybe she should have been on medication of some kind."

Julie put her arms around Tom and rubbed his back. "Honey, she seems to be doing well on her own and I know she let Mark stay close. That's a good sign. Not everyone needs meds and often, the symptoms disappear in time.

"She's tough," said Tom. "She's gone through hell and wouldn't let any of us help. That didn't make sense to me."

"It made sense to her. Trust me. She's normal. I wonder if she feels guilty that she survived and Pat was killed."

"That's something you could ask her if she wants to confide in you. Mom knows this is your expertise."

Emily came down the hall, caught sight of them and smiled. "Where's the food?"

It was a fine day for the visit with her children.

Tom returned from the supermarket with a car full of groceries. Within an hour, he had a sumptuous dinner cooking. Poached salmon simmered, shrimp was cleaned and on ice while he made cocktail sauce, and bacon-wrapped filet mignon marinated in a delicate soy, garlic, and ginger sauce. His hands flew as he chopped, diced, and worked magic with the vegetables.

Julie set the long table in the dining room with a white lace cloth that allowed the dark polished wood to shine through. She transformed linen napkins into fans and placed them upright in tall crystal glasses. Emily stood between the two rooms and watched with pleasure as the kids took over, her head swiveling as she observed one and then the other like watching a tennis match.

"Aside from the fact that we're together after a month, is there a special celebration going on that I'm not aware of?"

Julie ran past Emily, silky black hair flying, planted a kiss on Tom's cheek, and returned to her task in the dining room. "Just being with you is enough," she said.

A horn blared in the driveway. Emily hurried to open the door. Meg carefully climbed the steps, arms outstretched to greet her mother.

"Mom." She held her at arm's length for a moment before hugging her. "We didn't know what to expect, but you look pretty good. A little thin but I always say that." She laughed with relief. "Oh, Mom. It's so good to see you."

"Hi, my baby. Speaking of baby, it's my turn to inspect you," said Emily.

An expanded waist showed through the loose pink sweater worn over faded shorts. Meg sparkled with good health.

"We got through the first trimester, Mom" said Jake as he swaggered over, threw a proprietary arm around Meg's shoulder and planted a kiss on his mother-in-law's cheek.

"Isn't he goofy, Mom? He's like the alpha male you warned me about when I was a teenager."

"Hi Jake," said Emily. "It's good to see you. I can tell you're taking care of my treasure."

"Sure, Mom. It's my job. I'll never forget what you said when Meg brought me home the first time."

Emily was puzzled. "The only thing I remember from that day was when you walked in the house. My first thought was that Meg reeled in a big one. Then I wondered how you'd get your shoulders through the doorway."

"He lifted weights in those days, Mom," said Meg.

"Refresh my memory, Jake. What did I say that made such an impression?"

"You said take care of my daughter or you'll have to answer to me."

Emily was surprised. "I don't remember saying that. I didn't even know how to protect myself then."

"What are you saying?" said Meg, looking at her Mom. "You taught me it was wrong to step on a bug."

Emily snapped back. "It wasn't a bug who killed Pat."

The sudden outburst surprised Meg and Jake.

"Sorry, kids. My anger is close to the surface." She hugged them and the tension eased. "Come on in. You'll be happy to know that Tom is our caterer tonight."

"Great. Not that we don't love your cooking, Mom."

"Yeah, yeah, yeah," said Emily. "I'm famous for my gourmet peanut butter on toast."

Just then Mike and Amanda pulled up. The circle was complete. Ever the gentleman, Mike got out of the car, ran to the passenger side and gallantly helped his wife out. A radiant Amanda stepped from the car. She looked as though she could carry Mike.

Emily ran to greet Pat's daughter and son-in-law. "Hi, you two. Everyone's here now and Tom's cooking."

Cheers from Mandy and Michael. "Nothing personal, Mom, but just thinking about Tom turned loose in the kitchen makes my mouth water," said Mandy.

"So you haven't had morning sickness?" said Emily.

"No, but Michael has. I feed him saltine crackers and that helps."

"I never heard of a man with morning sickness," said Emily.

Mandy sailed up the steps. Over her shoulder she said, "It's called role reversal, Mom. He'll get over it."

Mike followed with their bags, a sheepish grin on his face. Emily shook her head. The visit had just begun and already it was full of surprises.

"Pass the salmon, please," Emily said as she sipped Chardonnay and bit into a sesame cracker. "One more taste before moving on to the next course."

Contented murmurs from the kids, knives and forks clinking against china. They ignored her request.

"Hello," she called. "Is it too much to ask for someone, anyone to listen to a mother and pass the salmon?"

"Yes," they chorused and continued eating.

"Thanks a bunch, gang." Emily stood, marched to the end of the table and helped herself to the remains of the salmon. "You're all out of the will." She finished a few morsels and reached for the sliced steak.

Tousled heads lifted from dining, forks in mid air. "What will?" Mike said.

She made them wait as she had while she slowly chewed a piece of meat and purred in appreciation. "Yum, Tom. Do leave the recipe for the marinade. I may decide to cook some day." She looked up at the expectant faces. "The will I haven't written yet." She returned to the serious business of eating.

Mike cleared his throat. "As spokesman for the gang, we apologize for rude behavior, Mom."

Emily looked from face to sheepish face. Sweet kids. "Apology accepted. Great dinner, Tom."

They began to clear the table to make room for dessert. Time for the seventh inning stretch. Emily leaned back and watched the flurry of activity she didn't have to participate in. Nice to be the observer after all the years of being the director. Rain drops hit the windows, a slow patter changed to a downpour. April showers.

No one listened as they chatted among themselves, passing plates and silverware.

"I'm opening a whorehouse. I'll be the madam." Emily poured coffee and watched steam rise in the delicate porcelain cup.

Tom dropped a knife. It skittered across the polished floor. "What?" Everyone stopped what they were doing. "Did you say whorehouse?"

"Yes, I did." Emily smiled..."Had to get your attention some way."

Again with the "Sorry, Mom."

"If you hurry up, clear the table, bring dessert and listen for a change, for God sakes, I may tell you."

Like cartoon figures, they moved fast and a few minutes later they had brownies and ice cream and listened to the Mother who had more things to talk about than they ever dreamed she was capable of.

Emily refilled her coffee cup offering the pot around to her children and relished being in the spotlight for once. They weren't interested in coffee. They were interested in what she had to say. Meg, face rounded with pregnancy, resembling less a girl and more a woman now, taking a fresh look at her Mom. Jake next to her, shoulders touching, patient as always. Tom, written on his expressive face, "Are you my Mother?" like the book she read to him when he was little. Wise-beyond-her-years Julie, expression read, "You go, Mom." Michael saw a change in his mother-in-law and Amanda patted her tummy and didn't get it.

A rumble of thunder followed by flashes of lightning was seen through the expanse of windows. A fanfare? Emily wondered as she revealed a period of change to the family.

"Mark suggested I move out for a while until they catch the man who killed Pat. He said this person seems to be obsessed with me for some reason and I'll be safer somewhere else. Short term. The police are closer every day."

Everyone talked at once asking where she would go, more about the suspect and so on. Emily explained as best she could. "So I wanted us to get together tonight. I won't be far since I start work Monday. The coach subbing for me is nice but not what the girls need. After dessert, I have something for you and then home you go."

"Pass the brownie, Meg," Tom said. He put a hand out for the plate.

"Say please, brat." said Meg.

"Please brat." Tom reached across Meg and grabbed the plate. Jake's hand shot out, stopping him.

"Some courtesy, bro." said Jake.

Emily didn't have to intervene. She loved it. "I'll leave you lovely folks to clean up. When you're through, please join me in the family room before you have to leave."

Emily listened to the clatter of the three couples cleaning up after dinner. Happy sounds. She didn't have to call out play nice, don't fight. She didn't have to do anything. Lovely to walk away from dishes. Those days were over. She curled up in her favorite rattan chair facing the window. The patio lights were on. The companion rockers on the patio glistened with raindrops that flew off as they moved in rhythm with the night wind. It was almost Easter. She sat alone as a spectator, no longer a participant with a mate. What's next?

The dishwasher began the first cycle.

The kids piled in the spacious room, conversations in progress.

"Why are you sitting in the dark?" said Tom. He placed a lap throw over her.

She smiled and flung it back at him. "It's seventy degrees tonight, Tom. Two things, kids. First, I'm in the dark because I enjoy the scenery in the lighted patio. And second, please don't treat me as if I were a fragile flower about to wilt."

The kids laughed, Tom the loudest.

"I guess that's my feeble attempt to shelter you," said Tom.

"Thanks, honey. Just treat me the way you always have."

"Oh. Okay. Mom, I need money, keys to the car, here's my laundry, see ya later."

Everyone broke up.

They settled down, looked out the window, and saw what captured their Mom's attention. The chairs.

"You miss my Dad," said Amanda. She reached over and touched Emily's hand. Her fingers curled around fingers her father had loved.

"Of course I do. Just as you do." Emily was pensive and asked, "Does anyone believe in resurrection?"

She observed their expressions, some puzzled at her question, some thoughtful.

"I believe in reincarnation," said Meg.

"Like what? You'll die and come back as a cute puppy?" said Tom.

Meg jumped to her feet, prepared to smack him.

"Play nice and don't fight," said Emily before she could stop the words.

Once more the group broke up with laughter.

"This was supposed to be a serious discussion—spiritual, philosophical, and deep," said Emily. "Somehow, it's deteriorated fast."

"Sorry about the insensitive rudeness, Meg and Mom," said Tom.

"What do you believe in, Mom?" said Mike.

"Thanks for asking, Mike. When my mother died suddenly at age fifty one, I looked at her and then I looked all around the room for wherever she might be. I knew she wasn't in her body anymore but her personality, her spirit had to be somewhere. That was my first experience as an adult losing someone I loved. I was twenty nine. I've felt her presence many times over the years especially when I was in danger."

"When was that?" Jake said.

"When I gave birth to Meg. Ask her later, okay?" Jake pulled his wife close to him. "I hear Pat's voice in my head, guiding me when I practice martial arts. I know in my heart, he'll be near when I need him. So, as terrible as this loss is, I feel we never completely lose our dearest ones and someday we'll be together."

"Wow. That's powerful stuff," said Tom.

"It gives me hope," said Amanda.

"Is there something specific on your mind, Mom," said Julie.

"Well, yes. I told you a month ago, I would give Pat's ashes to anyone who wanted some. Before you leave, I want to show you the urn they're in. It's a jar I made a few years ago." Emily stood up and beckoned to the gathering. "Don't be afraid. This is part of nature. You've heard the expression, ashes to ashes?" A few shrugs, mostly they looked blank. "It's the cycle of life. There's nothing to fear and it can be comforting."

They followed Emily to the living room. She picked up a large ceramic jar and showed it to them.

"I made smaller jars with stopper lids at the same time I made this one, never dreaming some day they'd be put to this use." She indicated four identical ceramic miniatures on the fireplace hearth. They were in a line, like children waiting for a treat.

"They're lovely, Mom. I didn't know you made pottery," Amanda said.

"I used to. I have all the equipment. If you want to learn, I'd love to teach you."

Emily spread newspaper on the hearth. She placed the large jar on top.

"Help yourself."

A hush fell over the group. Jake took Meg's hand and made the first move. The miniature jar was almost swallowed up by his large hand. With a delicacy not often seen, he scooped some ash into the jar using a small garden tool, without spilling any. He and Meg kissed Mandy's cheek and made room for Tom and Julie. After she picked up the remaining jars, one at a time, Julie selected the one that felt right to her and Tom filled it. They followed the example set by Jake and Meg and kissed Mandy's cheek. Tom threw in a big hug as well.

Mandy held Michael's hand and as they approached the large urn, her tears welled up and fell. Mike placed a jar in her shaking hand.

"Do you want me to fill it, honey?"

She shook her head. "No. I can do it." Mandy put her hand into the urn. "Hi, Dad," she said in a soft voice. She trickled ash through her fingers. Some ash fell on her sweater. Startled, she looked at Emily.

"It's okay, Mandy," said Emily. "This is for good luck from your Dad and from all of us.

Emily came out of the ladies room dressed in a bikini. She

finally got together with her best friends for tennis and lunch

"Look at you, girlfriend. Not only are you devoid of one ounce of extra fat, but your muscles have muscles," Margaret said, always engaged in the battle of the bulge. "How do you do that?"

"Grief agrees with me, I guess," Emily said.

As she went into the whirlpool room to wait for them, she overheard Ginny say, "What can we do for her?"

"She said she'd talk after tennis and she will. Hurry before she changes her mind," Shelly said.

Emily sat alone in the hot water, steam rose all around her. Her hand waved through a wisp of steam. The door opened, the wisps danced and settled in the disturbed air. Time for a chat with women she'd known since childhood.

Margaret, Jesse, and Shelly eased into the water and surrounded Emily, the hub of the wheel in this circle of friends. Jesse set the timer for twenty minutes. Bubbles sprang into action, strategically placed jets pulsed and brought comfort to aches and pains. Her friends waited.

"When Larry died suddenly," Emily spoke in a soft steady voice, "I should've left well enough alone. A happy marriage of thirty years is almost more than a person could ask for. Should've, would've, could've."

The women leaned toward Emily to hear every word over the noise of the pool.

"So I meet this man, great on the exterior, damaged on the interior where it doesn't show, like day old bread or seconds you can buy for less at a discount store. But who's to know? That's a rhetorical question. No answer required."

She smiled. Her friends nodded.

"I want companionship, he's starved for love. And the sex is incredible. He's a walking hard-on."

In spite of themselves, everyone broke-up except Emily.

"Our time together is one long orgasm." She glanced at her friends. "Do you know what I mean?"

No one did.

"So we get married and before too long, I'm learning martial arts. And loving it. He wants me to learn how to protect myself and now I believe I can." Surprised looks from the women.

"Yes, I now have an orange belt and continue to work on my

skills." She talked faster and faster.

"He installs a fancy burglar alarm system that makes my house on the beach as safe as the White House, and I don't see my buddies too often because he keeps me so busy."

She paused for a breath as her train of thought peaked at the top of a mountain and hurtled down without stop. She's barely visible; they're all barely visible in the heat and steam from the pulsing whirlpool as the timer moved on.

"And when I accuse him of controlling me, he's distraught, begs my forgiveness, promises to stop— how did he put it?" She searched for his words in the mist. "Yes. He'll stop looking in his rearview mirror before he loses what's right in front of him. Nice, huh? So I forgive him and we go for a run early one morning and I run very fast and he lags behind. Suddenly a stranger appears, almost touches me, Pat's not around, I think he's way back but when I turn, he's nowhere in sight. So I run and run...and find him in the water. Dead. Killed by hit and run, the man cops are searching for as we speak. I'm a widow again."

The timer clicked off, the bubbles slowed and disappeared. The steam dissipated.

"And that's what happened."

Emily was dry-eyed. Tears streamed down the faces of her friends.

Her voice steady as she finished, Emily said, "I never should've let him into my life."

"Now who's looking in the rearview mirror?" Jesse said.

"One more thing. Did you love him?" Shelly said.

Emily didn't miss a beat. "Yes, oh yes."

Margaret wrapped up in a towel and wiped her eyes. "One long orgasm?"

The mood was broken.

Chapter 24

Routine was a wonderful thing. Coaching today, the girls happy she returned, jumping hurdles, and sweating. What a great way to spend the morning and get paid for it. She had to get them in shape for the trials coming up. The bus pulled away and for a moment, Emily was sad. Then she grabbed her gear and jogged home.

After lunch Emily sat on the floor in Pat's office engaged in a stare-down with the VCR. It was off but she felt it was alive, the recorded tape demanding to be turned on. She weighed the value of keeping the scenes to replay at another time; her hand flicked the rewind button and hit record. The pictures were history. Motion sensors would record over them. Emily sighed with regret.

The phone rang. Her body on automatic, she picked it up.

"John O'Keefe, Mrs. Corwin. I wanted to give you a heads up. One of my men found a coffee cup on one of the dunes near the back of your house. It was mostly covered by sand but we recovered prints and have a positive I.D. Has a man, Clifford Lansdale, ever been a guest in your home?"

Shocked and frightened, Emily said, "No but he was my husband's client not so long ago. Pat successfully defended him in a big case."

"Yes, we know that. He was never in your home socially?"

"No. I never met him. Never even saw a picture of him."

"I better come over with a photo. We have an APB out on him, Mrs. Corwin. Please stay at home, doors locked until further notice. A police watch is already posted. Goodbye."

Fear raced through her. He's on the loose and he wants her. Oh my God and Mark won't be back from his trip for another hour. Okay, okay. Emily turned on all the lights in the house, breathing deeply as she went from room to room. All she had was herself right now. She ran up the stairs, dressed in her Ge, went through

Kata movements, kicks, blocks, and thought of 'The way of the foot and fist.' She thought of a male attacker and what she, a smaller person, could do to protect herself. When every step was in place and she felt in control, she left her own little Dojo upstairs.

When Officer O'Keefe rang the chimes, he was surprised to find Emily Corwin dressed in a white uniform, orange belt wrapped around her narrow waist, a look of resolve on her face.

She identified the photo as the stranger at the beach. Absolutely.

The phone rang.

"Hi Mark."

"Am I that predictable?" he said.

"I've had my eye on the clock all day, hoping your flight left Los Angeles on time and I'd hear from you around eight o'clock. It's now exactly eight and we're on the phone. Are we in the same state?"

"Yes. In fact, I'll be at your door in less than fifteen minutes."

"Great. I've so much to tell you, you'll get tired of my voice." Emily didn't want to fill him in about Clifford Lansdale. It could wait until he arrived. There was a knock at the back slider doors. "Someone's at the door. See you in a few. 'Bye."

Who's at my door at this hour? She walked down the hall, turning more lights on as she went. Suddenly she stopped and turned back. A feeling, a sense of someone behind her.

"Pat?" She moved in a circle, arms extended with palms up. "Pat, are you here?" Nothing, yet a strong feeling of him persisted. Persistent knocking.

"I'm coming."

It's the guard John said was going to here, she thought. A uniformed man with broad shoulders waited impatiently.

"Is something wrong?" Without thinking, she unlocked the door, recognized the man and ran. He was in her home. Oh God. He slid the door wide open, raced to catch up with her, grabbed her around the waist and dragged her back toward the gaping door. She knew he wanted to get her out, out to the beach where he was free to do whatever he intended all this time. And he was powerful, much stronger than she. A tank compared to a tricycle.

Now he had her under the arms, pulling her across the threshold out on the patio, as she kicked and screamed. But the ocean roared back and covered her screams and now they were on the old wooden path to the beach. She tried to dig in with her heels, to twist in his grip, what else could she do? Her fingers dragged along, sifting for a weapon, a shell, a loose board. Nothing.

Close to the water's edge he let go and stood above her one foot one her chest, roaring like a lion with his prize. Big mistake, Emily's mind registered. You're mine.

A quick twist of her body, she grabbed his leg and kicked it from under him. He howled with rage and she kicked him again and danced away. Taught to hurt a larger opponent and run screaming for help wasn't going to work for her. He had something else on his mind and so did Emily. An eye for an eye.

She ran but his long legs were after her through splashing waves, the incoming tide. Long arms again grabbed her from behind, held tight across her waist. What was he saying? "Goddess, you're mine now." Emily stomped as hard as she could on his bare feet at the same time slamming her head up and back into his face. He dropped his hands in pain, fell backward and she ran screaming toward her home. Screaming for help as loud as she could. And help was there, running, guns out, and Mark was there. Mark picked her up and held her against the chill and terrors of the night.

"Mark. Oh Mark." She began to cry.

"I'm sure you noticed the security cameras in this room. The attack would be recorded on a tape. Do you want me to take it out?" Mark said to John O'Keefe.

"Don't touch it. I'll get the tape when the team finishes."

An involuntary shudder passed through her. "Will I ever be all right?" Dressed in dry sweats an extra blanket wrapped around her, Emily spoke softly to Mark.

"After what you've been through tonight, you deserve a medal. You are more than all right. And you battled that man by yourself, a man twice your size." He hugged her gently. She was bruised. Legs, arms, sweet face.

"The evidence is captured on tape. I'll make a copy and give one to the police."

A bottle of Chardonnay in an ice bucket was on the counter, two crystal glasses beside it, next to a tray with cheese and rice crackers.

"You had this ready for my arrival. So thoughtful of you." He opened the bottle and poured a glass for her. "This might calm you."

She took the glass from him, her eyes vacant, empty. "That's what scares me. Deep inside, I am calm." She watched the wine sway in the glass. She inhaled shallow, quick breaths and tried not to cry. "Maybe I'm not so calm."

Mark held her by the shoulders, turned her face to his. "Listen to me. You're in shock. Thank God you trained in self defense. I thought it was excessive protection, but something inside you knew better."

She sipped the wine. It had no taste.

"Are you ready to talk now before Officer O'Keefe comes in?"

"Not really, but I'll try."

"Tell me exactly what happened. When I called fifteen minutes ago, you had to hang up. You said someone was at the door." She nodded. "Then what happened?"

She told him as much as she remembered. He was obviously upset to hear every word. Jaw clenched, he paced the floor and John O'Keefe entered.

"Are you all right, Mrs. Corwin? You nailed the bast...him. He's going away forever. Assaulting a police officer added to his crimes. He bashed the man guarding the back door, wore his uniform to get in and the rest is history. But you're the hero. I don't know how you did it." He shook her hand. "I'm ready for the tape and we're out of here."

Unbidden, images from Pat's funeral flooded her mind. Her eyes shut tight. Samuel's strong arms, kisses on both cheeks, whispers. *What did he say? An eye for an eye.* Mark's voice invaded the memory. "What is it?"

Her eyes blinked open. "An eye for an eye, Mark."

"Don't say those words to anyone but me, please. His voice was intense.

"Just a minute," said Mark. "Why don't you clean up while I get the tape?"

He escorted her to the bedroom. She didn't turn her head, grateful that he protected her.

"Do you plan to stay here tonight?"

"No." She felt so cold. "Not tonight."

"Pack a bag. We'll leave after they do, all right?" She nodded.

He called to the officer. "Follow me. I'm going to make a copy of the tape for my records. You can have the original, okay?"

"Sure."

Mark handed over the tape. "If you have any questions after viewing the tape, please call me." He gave him a business card.

They walked to the front door.

Footsteps down the hall, Mark coming. Fast, slower and slower still. Emily packed and ready. She peered at the doorway through swollen eyes, make-up applied with care hours before now streaked, hair tangled. Why didn't he come rushing in, sweep her off her feet, carry her off? A damsel in distress picture came to her mind and she almost laughed. Almost. Not this Emily. The old Emily would have welcomed the knight in whatever armor he had to rescue her. Maybe Mark decided he didn't like the new Emily. Maybe he liked the compliant Goody Two Shoes of yesterday. Maybe — She straightened up, pushed back wet hair that refused to obey and called to him.

"Mark, I hope that's you in the hall. I'm only good for one self-defense a day at this point," voice light as she spoke. She didn't feel light.

To her surprise a disheveled Mark showed up at the door and stopped, as if he were afraid to enter the bedroom without an invitation, confidence of a little while ago gone. The take-charge facade he displayed to the world had peeled away to reveal the young man she knew years ago when he was in law school.

She held out her arms and he stumbled into them. "Hold me tight, please. I feel as if I'm coming apart at the seams," he said. She stroked his back, rubbed tight muscles in his neck. "As I drove here from the airport, all I thought about was you, how much I care for you, how this time there was a chance for us to have a life together, to grow old together." He inhaled a long shuddering breath. "From a distance I saw flashing lights, knew something

189

terrible —" hoarse sobs, "when I saw you standing, soaked but standing on the beach I almost lost it. Relief sure, but that thing at your feet, he attempted to kill — my precious Emily." He pulled away and cradled her face with both hands.

"Don't look too close, Mark. I'm a mess." She couldn't help herself and added, "You should've seen the other guy." He did a double-take. "Sorry. A little black humor. Helps me through the bad times. This qualifies, don't you think?"

He sat down in the only chair and pulled her onto his lap. "Your sense of humor is big enough for the two of us. Will you share it with me?"

As an answer, she hugged him and rested her head in the crook of his neck. After a while she said, "How many times have you held me like this since Pat died?"

"Who's counting?"

In the quiet house, chilly from the front door left open for so long, they warmed each other with body heat.

"Right now, I want to get out of here fast. I'll shower and finish packing ."

She eased off his lap and crossed to the mirror. There were blood caked scratches on her arms and cheeks. Not pretty. Mark's reflection in the mirror spoke to her. "You're a survivor and you're beautiful. You faced an enemy and survived."

She looked around the bedroom and searched for a sign of Pat. There was none.

Her voice grew stronger. "Mark, Pat's gone and he's coming not back. And that's okay."

A few tears escaped and rolled down his cheeks. "I'll always be grateful to him."

After showering, Emily finished packing and walked out of the room, hitting lights as she went, a path of darkness left in her wake. Mark waited in the kitchen. He packed the Jarlsberg cheese and wine in a bag and searched the refrigerator for anything else she might want.

"Carrots?" he said, as he withdrew baby carrots from the vegetable drawer.

"Okay."

"Let me carry that, lady," he said in a deep voice, and pried the overnight bag from her hand.

"I can do it," she protested. "I'm strong." She rolled up her sleeve to reveal a tight bicep. "See."

Mark smiled, a dimple flashed, "I know you are. I just like helping out once in a while. Is that all right?"

She smiled back. "I guess so."

Click, click and more lights went out or were dimmed as Emily wanted. Outdoor grounds lights were on a timer. One last glance at the rocking chairs, she turned her back on them, hit the security code, the red light glowed. Odd. It no longer had an evil look.

Emily slammed the door and called to Mark, "Now what were you saying about a place for me to stay?"

Book Club Discussion Starters

Starting Over

By Charmaine Gordon

- Starting over after you've been with a mate for many years is difficult. Emily had to juggle her family and friends to fit Patrick Corwin into her life. Have you been in the same or similar situation?

- Do you think she handled her children as well as she might have?

- The older you are, the more complicated life gets. Her long time friend, widower Mark Wagner wants to get together and she's already committed to Pat. What would you do?

- In Shakespeare's plays, there is always a parallel story. Starting Over's parallel tale is Clifford Lansdale, a psychopath who stalks Emily and finds his own lawyer is the man who wins her love. Ask yourself the question. If the one who loves you insists you learn self defense, would you take the time to learn because someday that knowledge might save your life?

- Could you fight to save yourself if threatened?

- Do you believe in an eye for eye to get justice?

More Great Books by Charmaine Gordon

The Catch

Tom Donnelly, once known as The Catch – every woman's dream guy, has fallen down every rung of the ladder he once worked so hard to climb. On New Year's Day, he realizes just how far he's fallen, and makes a list of resolutions to change his life. He vows to regain the trust lost from his family, his law firm, and his friends – and maybe even find the right woman this time.

Sin of Omission

A twist of fate intervenes when Shelley keeps a secret that threatens to break apart the Costigans and her future. A mysterious client, Deanna Rose, enters Haven, victim of a savage beating under strange circumstances. Shelley investigates and finds Ms. Rose has an unsavory past. With the reputation and safety of Haven at stake, Shelley is at risk to lose everything and everyone she cares about.

Reconstructing Charlie

Charlie Costigan has a secret. Home life gone from bad to the worst when she protects her mother from another vicious attack by her drunken father. Midnight. Clothes thrown into an old suitcase, she races for the bus with a letter to an unknown aunt and uncle. "This is my daughter. Embrace her as if she were your own." Determined, Charlie begins again. Alone with her secret.

Now What?

I held his cooling hand and asked the two words spoken many times during our years together. "Now what?" This time there was no response. I was on my own for the first time. When my fingers touched his wedding ring, I slipped it off and held it in my fist. The gold band was warm. I clung to him. "Come back to me, dearest." Sometimes what you wish for is more than you can live with.

Starting Over
Each morning, Emily Kendrick runs on the hard-packed sand of St. Augustine Beach to clear her mind and heal her heart. From the widow's walk of the house perched high on the dunes, a man trains his binoculars on Emily...

 **ALSO IN AUDIOBOOK!**

To Be Continued
Elizabeth Malone wakes up the morning after an amazing night of passion with her husband of forty years to find a note: Dear Lizzie, it's not you, it's me. Abandoned by her husband, disappointed in daughter Susie's casual attitude Dad's having a mid-life crisis, Beth decides to re-establish herself as the winner she once was. When Frank Malone returns, he's in for a big surprise!

The first three stories in the series of Mature Romance combined in one volume. *Instant Grandpa*, Book 1; *Young at Heart*, Book 2; and *Before the Final Curtain*, Book 3. Charmaine Gordon stories of love, passion, and suspense starring sexy seniors.

Instant Grandpa, Book 1
Summer at the Jersey Shore just got hotter... Take one widower grandfather, add two little grandkids, and widowed grandmother with a small granddaughter. Mix well. Stir in sun drenched beach days and moonlit nights. What have you got? A kite flying high with a new tail; an author writing a book to sort out emotions; a talented boy with his mother returned to claim the prize.

Young at Heart, Book 2
Seventy year old Joyce Campbell expected her new left hip to heal at Helen Hayes Rehabilitation. What she didn't expect was to fall in love with the distinguished silver haired Collin Brody who wouldn't give her a second glance. Until Kizzy, the therapy dog comes into Collin's life...and into his heart. What happens next? The Beginning, Not the End.

Before the Final Curtain, Book 3
Once lovers, aging actors collide on stage as stars in a romantic comedy written and directed by a manipulative director. Add to the mix the talented assistant, a tough stage manager, one prominent costume designer, two young actors, secrets and gossip. Show business. There's no business like it.

Charmaine Gordon writes books about women who Survive and Thrive. Her motto is take one step and then another to leave your past behind and begin again. Six books and several short stories in three years, she's always at work on the next story. The books include *To Be Continued, Starting Over, Now What?, Reconstructing Charlie, Sin of Omission* and *The Catch*, just released.

"I didn't realize at the time while working as an actor in NYC, I'd become a sponge soaking up dialogue, setting, and stage directions. I learned many tools of writing during the years watching directors like Mike Nichols and actors including Harrison Ford, Anthony Hopkins, and Billy Crystal. And would you believe, I was Geraldine Ferraro's stand-in leg model, my first job giving me entrée into all the Unions needed to work. When the sweet time ended, I began another career and creative juices flowed."

You can reach Charmaine at
http://authorCharmaineGordon.wordpress.com

And on her FB page
http://www.facebook.com/charmaine.gordon